Fast Forward
and
Other Stories

DELIA DE SANTIS

LONGBRIDGE BOOKS

Legal Deposit
National Library of Canada

Library and Archives Canada Cataloguing in Publication

De Santis, Delia, 1943-
       Fast forward : and other stories / Delia De Santis.

ISBN 978-0-9809700-0-5

       I. Title.

PS8607.E75155F38 2008   C813'.6   C2008-901797-8

Published by Longbridge Books
P.O. Box 695
Jean-Talon Postal Station
Montreal, Quebec, H1S 2Z5

longbridgebooks@gmail.com

Printed in Canada
Cover painting: Ezio De Santis, *Activity A*

For
Antonia
and
in memory of
Saverio

Contents

Fast Forward 9

Call Display 19

Abandoned Wedding Ring 25

The Blue House 29

The Last Frozen Dinner 33

Snow on the Roofs 43

Blueberry Muffins 45

A Little Visiting 49

Before the Roses Fade 59

A Place I Once Knew 65

No Man of Music 69

Faces in the Window 83

Cinzia 87

The Vineyard 95

Before You Leave 99

Visions 103

Don't Forget Tomorrow 109

Talk About Roses 113

The House My Father Built 119

Nothing Changes 121

A Garden of Soft Colours 127

Ant Hills 137

Another Time, Another Day 143

The Last Time 147

Fast Forward

I am coming back from the corner store when she pulls into her driveway, between my house and hers. She opens the back door of her car and, before bending down toward the seat to pick up a grocery bag, she motions for me to wait.

"Well, hi," she says, as she straightens up, "I just wanted to introduce myself. I am Eufemia. Spelled with an "f" – Italian… And I thought that if you're bored sometimes in the evening, you could come over for tea or coffee. I never made friends with the lady who lived there before… but you seem different. Of course," she is quick to add, "you might not want to make friends with me."

She's at least ten years younger than I am. Her hair is dark and straight, her features blunt in a most appealing kind of way. As a young girl she would have had the kind of face you see on posters of children left homeless, orphans.

"No, no… tea would be great – or coffee. I drink anything. And it also seems that we already have something in common. We're both Italian."

"Oh, I know," she laughs.

"How did you know?" I say, wondering about it, since I don't look at all Italian. My mother is from Trieste and my father from a village by the French border. I have high cheekbones and my hair is fire red, my skin milky white. So much mixing of blood over the years.

"I heard you swearing in Italian last night, when you were trying to open your kitchen window." Then she casts a glance toward my arm – I am wearing my Gucci watch. "I bet you're not used to sliders," she grins, with an intuitive look about her. "I bet you're used to crank windows. Makes a difference."

"As long as you don't lose the handles," I laugh, and right away I decide to tell her about my situation, which she seems to have partly guessed already.

"Yeah, well, since my husband and I split up I've had to change my lifestyle. I got the matrimonial house, but I had to lease it out, as I have no other income. We used to live in the north end – Silver Lake."

I expect her to say something about Silver Lake. Everyone knows that's where the castles and the villas are – the homes some people call "monster houses." But when she speaks again I know her mind has bypassed all that.

"I never had a husband," she murmurs. "Never a man of my own. Not even a live-in boyfriend."

I haven't told her my name yet, but I know it's a thing that can wait. No need to intrude just now and steal the moment from her. An expression of sweet sorrow has settled on her face.

●●●

I never used to tell my affluent friends certain things in life. But then, they were the kind of friends who would not go the length to keep up a friendship with me. They don't refuse to come and visit me now, but in their carefully selected words, they put me off by saying it's easier if I go to Silver Lake to see them instead.

There's *everything* there, they say - everything to do - everything to keep one entertained. And before I can even begin to explain that I can't afford certain social recreations anymore, they're right back to mixing their drinks and talk of tennis.

"Wow," says Eufemia, after listening to my story of how I had finally kicked Carlo out. It's about a month after our initial meeting, and we're on her back porch, sharing barbecued sausages and a radicchio salad. "How did you plan it all ... to kick him out like that? It must have taken you days to rehearse it ... just the two of you on his birthday ... and then poof, 'Get out or I'll poison you.'"

"Eufemia," I say, shaking my head. "You watch too many movies. It makes you distort things. It wasn't like that at all. What I told you is that I *felt* like poisoning him. That's a different thing altogether. Anyway, deep down I wanted to win him back, if you can believe it. That's how it started out. I knew all about the other women, but still I wanted to hold on to him. Crazy, I know."

She laughs. "The big cash flow - lifestyle."

"Oh shut up," I say. "What do you know?"

"If you're referring to love ... *nada*, my friend. Sweet nothing."

Later, we go inside to watch *The Horse Whisperer.* She has seen the movie four times already. I had to go and rent it for her - she was too embarrassed to go herself. At the local video store they all know her, and she doesn't want them thinking she's weird.

"Look," I say, watching her leaf through a magazine. "If you're not looking at the screen, why rent the bloody thing again?"

"I know, but there's that one scene I'm waiting for ... when they're dancing - Redford and her."

"Fast forward then," I say, annoyed. It wasn't my first time seeing the movie, either.

"No. I need to wait ... one needs to go through what comes first."

Yeah, like a bad marriage, I think to myself.

"It's very important," she continues absently, "what comes before."

I think about that for a moment. "Well, I suppose it does make sense. In certain circumstances, it does shape our lives."

Then I look at her. She's really beautiful, and I can't believe that no man ever wanted to marry her. Has it been her fault, I wonder? Eufemia always waiting for the right moment, needing the anticipation, the scenes which give way to the momentum – never living for the moment, because maybe it wasn't just right yet?

Finally, the scene.

"It's how he touches her. My God, it's to die for. A thousand deaths."

I want to tell her that he's not touching her ... he's *holding* her. But I know I could never get Eufemia's attention right now. She's too caught up in what is taking place on the screen, the storybook life of a man and a woman.

Just then I think of my mother. Of how she had once told me with tears in her eyes that my father had never put his arms around her in front of people. Then I think of my father – now dead for three years – his quiet, reserved manner ... the way he sometimes watched my mother move around the kitchen, *holding* her with his eyes.

What more did my mother want? She had what the actor on the screen is giving ... and she didn't have it only for a moment, but a lifetime – and my father's love was real.

● ● ●

Eufemia has weekends off, and on those two days she becomes a real pest. I know it's her at the door again – third time since morning. She never uses the doorbell; she likes to knock. She says it's more personal, intimate, and I have to admit she's right. I can actually tell what mood she's in as soon as her knuckles hit the door, the way the sound reverberates through the hollow wood panel.

Tonight she's excited about something - I can sense it. And the minute I open up, she pushes her way in.

"He was here," she exclaims, her eyes open wide, like a child's. "What took you so long at the mall? - he couldn't wait. I knew it was Carlo as soon as I saw the Jag pull up in your driveway. So I ran over and asked him if he was looking for you... Wow, is he ever a big man ... but charming. God, for a minute I thought he was going to kiss my hand!"

"Eufemia, stop it. The man would kiss a horse's ass, if - never mind. What's that you're waving in the air?"

"*This?*" She raises the envelope up high with excitement. "It's the letter he came to bring you."

• • •

I have locked myself in the bathroom and I am sobbing. Eufemia is on the other side and she's crying too, but for a different reason. She's scared about me, and she won't go away. She's afraid I'll do something crazy. I reach for a towel and make myself bite into a chunk of terry cloth, to choke my sobs down. And after a few minutes I am able to reassure her that I'll be all right. I tell her that slashing my wrists is the last thing on my mind.

"If that's true, swear on it then. Please, Gina," she begs.

"There's no Bible in here," I say, trying to make her laugh - and maybe myself too.

"Swear to anything ... the toilet bowl ... the sink. Just do it. Make a promise."

"You never give up, do you? Okay, I promise. And now you promise me you'll go to the store to buy a bottle of wine. I suddenly have a great big desire to get drunk tonight."

"Whatever was in that letter really got you upset, didn't it, Gina?"

13

I'd like to hit her over the head. And I will if she doesn't stop it, if she doesn't go away soon. "The wine," I say, "Merlot."

"I know… I know you don't want to talk about it."

"I didn't say that, Eufemia. You're just a pain in the butt. You need to learn to give people time, space… My God, the first day I met you, you even told me the spelling of your name, as if for some strange reason I was going to have to spell *Eufemia* the very next day."

"Well, what about you?" she retorts. "You even told me the *number* of times your husband had cheated on you… But never mind our personalities… I'll get two bottles instead of one, and I'll join you."

"Thank you. You're a real pal. And I am not being sarcastic."

"But you'll have to come over to my place. I can't hold *vino* the way you do. After two glasses, I won't be able to find my way home."

Home. That's what I had once. A home. But Carlo wrecked it. He spoiled the sacred institution of our marriage… and now he wants the structure too, the mortar and the bricks.

Over my dead body.

Later that evening, after wending my way back from Eufemia's house, feeling maudlin and not as drunk as I would have liked to be, I phone my mother. When her answering machine comes on, I hang up. But after a minute I dial again. I do that a few times, until the blessed woman answers.

"What's so important?" she complains. "I had to come out of the tub. Do you know what time it is?"

"Midnight. And all the good women should be in bed."

"I don't know what that is supposed to mean, Gina. Have you been drinking?"

"Drinking, yes. But not drunk enough. Of that I can surely assure you. Surely *shirly*."

"*Va bene*. What's wrong then? *Che è successo?* Something is wrong. I can tell."

"Mama," I suddenly blurt out, "I want you to come back home."

"And where is that?" she says quietly.

"You know where home is. Here in Canada. I want you to come back. I'll take care of you..."

"I am not sick, Gina. And to your surprise, I may still have quite a few years of good health."

"That's the whole thing. Where are all the friggin mothers of the world - tell me that? They're all down in Florida when you need them."

"Okay, Gina. Spit it out. Why are you in such an emotional state?"

"I am not in an emotional state!"

She gives a deep sigh. "All right, I'll come home. Obviously, it's something serious. I'll check on a flight tomorrow. I'll come as soon as I can."

"Forget it. I've changed my mind!"

"Okay, let's put it this way then... what has he done this time - Carlo? And anyway, whatever he's done shouldn't matter anymore. The two of you are divorced. You should have your separate lives."

"It's never over, Mother. Guess what he's up to now? The nerve of the man! He wants to buy the house back from me. He came around today ... brought a written offer."

"Uh," she says calmly, "I hope it's a good one. How much?"

"Seven hundred thousand."

"But the house isn't worth that much, or is it?"

"No, Mother, don't you see? He made me an offer I can't refuse."

"Well, accept it then."

"I can't. I won't. It's my house. *Mine.* I designed it. I picked out the tiles and the carpets, the cupboards, the counters; I sketched the fireplace mantle - everything. It's all me in that house. I will not let him have it."

"Take the offer, Gina. The house is too big a responsibility for you. I know the lease gives you a good income, but when that house starts needing a new roof, when things start going wrong with it - not just the money but the hassle... And what if when this lease is over, you can't get another one right away? What then? You'll have to pay taxes even on an empty house. How are you going to pay?"

"I'll get a job."

"A job, doing what? A part time Thanks-for-shopping-at-Kmart...? You will be in the poor house. I don't know why you didn't settle with cash. You've let pride put a big burden on your shoulders. But this is your chance to get out of it, so get out of it."

Suddenly I feel really weary. The weight of what my mother is saying is starting to settle over me, and I feel as if I am about to be buried under rocks. I take a deep breath; I need to scramble free.

"Well, if I have to sell it, I will. But damn it, Mother, I'll demand as much money as I want. I'll get everything I can out of him. I am not going to let that tramp he's going to marry benefit from anything that was mine."

"The girl is with child, Gina. Let things go. And let Carlo have his child in peace."

I dry sudden tears from my eyes and gulp the lump in my throat. "Yeah, but the bugger couldn't get me pregnant once in twenty seven years. And it wasn't my fault!"

"Oh, Gina."

"Yeah, and you can't imagine how much I wanted that man's child..."

I can't believe I've said that - and to my mother of all people. The revelation leaves me with a strange feeling in my chest, as though I have been emptied by being turned upside down.

Mama is silent on the other end. She is silent for a long time. But when she speaks again, she's still gentle. She says: "Gina, what are mothers for if not to be with their daughters...? You're right. It's about time I came to spend a winter at home."

After Mama hangs up, I press the phone to my cheek, as if the instrument were the dearest of objects.

● ● ●

I have seen the boxes in Eufemia's basement before, but this is the first time she has opened one to show me what's inside.

"Hats?" I say, surprised. "For God's sake."

"Yes, hats."

She tells me that years ago, when she was still living in Toronto, she worked in a hat factory and, often at the end of the week, the manager used to give out a box of hats to each of his favourite female workers. "The hats were *seconds*," she explains. And some of the young girls used to sell them to the mothers of their friends and get money for going to the movies and to dances, but she kept them all for herself.

"But why?"

"I don't know."

I shake my head. "You're crazy."

"It's the other way around. It's the hats that have kept me from going over the edge. When I feel really lonely, I come down here and try the hats on. Look at this one," she says, holding it up. "It's my favourite."

The hat is of a pretty ash colour and the material is like threads of fine silky straw. It's flexible and it can be bent this way and that. There's a tall mirror leaning on the wall and Eufemia goes to stand in front of it. She puts the hat on, and proceeds to show me a variety of transformations.

"Amazing."

17

"Not really. It's pretty simple."

"Okay," I say, an idea suddenly bursting in on me. "This is it. You're going to be my model…"

"For what?"

"Photographs. My new hobby - our new hobby. Maybe a profession. Who knows? Look, I used to be a photographer before I got married. Before I gave it all up to fatten up Carlo with his favourite Italian meals … and to play the perfect hostess to his business associates and their darling wives - me included… I never did tell you all that, did I?"

She gives a little sigh, and I wait for her to say something. I need her to say something. Anything.

At last she turns my way. "A lot of things you didn't tell me," she says, her face partially shadowed by the brim of the flexible hat; her features full of hidden drama. "But that's okay, because there are a lot of things I didn't tell you either … all the mistakes I made when I was younger…"

I don't know what makes me do it, but I lift my hand and I touch the tips of my fingers to her lips. I say: "Don't speak of it. Not now. Some things are better stretched over time…"

"And time could be years," she sighs, wistful but not sad.

"As in friendship," I smile, hurrying toward the stairs. "And don't you dare change your pose. I'll be back in an instant with my camera."

"Oh sure. As if I could hold a pose."

But I keep right on going, because I know that when I'll get back, Eufemia will be there waiting for me to snap the picture, the angle of her hat unchanged. I also know that we are both ready, as ready as we can ever be, to do what needs to be done to survive our failures.

Call Display

Giovanni meets his women in bars, late on weekend nights. He meets them the easy way; he goes over to them, or they come over to him. No sweat. Especially after he's had a few beers.

But lately he has begun to feel repulsion for his kind of life... a loathing of himself. More and more, he feels like a dog... a dog that has been rolling on grass he himself has soiled. There's clean grass on the other side, but the yard is fenced. He needs to find an open gate... or at least a gate that has been left unlocked, so that he can attempt to paw his way out.

He thinks of Lucia next door, a widow about his age - forty-five. If he were to describe her, he would say she's the kind of person who when washing her face forgets to look in the mirror ... and when brushing her hair often misses her bangs so that they're left standing straight. She's petite, dresses sensibly, and probably has a hard time finding shoes to fit her tiny feet.

The woman doesn't go around mourning her husband, but he can bet that every morning she wakes up to nice memories of the man she loved. Giovanni can picture her lifting the shirt tail of her pajamas to dry the tears from her eyes. Of course, she would quickly tell herself to smarten up, because feeling sorry for herself would not make things any better.

She wears white pajamas, one pair with little blue flowers and one with tiny pink ones. She wears no other colours - he knows - he sees her laundry on the line all the time. Lucia always puts her wash out in the summer ... and during the other seasons, too, when the days are half decent.

Giovanni has good looks and charm, and a face that never ages. But still, if he ever hopes to get anything going with Lucia, he will need to sharpen his approach, refine it. He has to relearn the ways of his youth, in the years when he was still hoping to find true love - before the sense of failure had set in, making him slowly succumb to the pleasures of the flesh, replacement for what was missing in his life. *Yes, he's fully aware that where Lucia is concerned he has to create and invent possibilities for fitting encounters. But how?*

In the two years he has been her neighbour, he has noticed that her outings consist only of short trips here and there in the neighbourhood; the grocery store, the drugstore, the post office, and the bank. Giovanni goes to the cleaners a lot, but he has never seen Lucia there; he's certain she washes her own good blouses, even if the label says "dry clean only." She's that kind of person. She goes to church, of course - he sees her every Sunday when she leaves - but that's one place he himself hasn't been to for a long time. He started to drift away when his sins began to get too complicated to tell a priest.

He could call her up - her number is in the phone book. But she probably has "call display" and on seeing his name appear on the little screen, she would never answer. He knows what most of the Italian people in town think of him, what they call him: Giovanni, *Don Giovanni.* That leaves very little to be inferred, even for people who don't know him.

Suddenly he remembers there's a way he can "block" his name and phone number; he can do it by pressing *67 before dialing. Then she wouldn't know who the caller was!

In the phone book, Lucia Donatelli's number is listed on page 93 - he still remembers from the first time he found himself looking it up. Slowly he begins to dial. But when he gets to the last two digits, he suddenly gets cold feet. He just cannot do it. Giovanni holds the phone in his hand for a long time although he knows the moment for making himself try again has long passed.

• • •

At the cleaners, he drops a bundle of clothes on the arborite counter. Antonio, the owner, says, "What's up, my friend? When do you need them back?"

"Next week... anytime. I don't care."

Antonio counts the items out loud. "Five pants, two jackets, and ten shirts - two suits. How many weddings do you think you're going to get invited to?" he chuckles. The two men have known each other for a long time.

"I hope none. I am going into a monastery - I am going to mothball the clothes."

Antonio lowers his glasses to the tip of his nose, peers at Giovanni with naked eyes. "Don't waste your money on moth balls. You won't last two months. Unless, of course, if there's a nunnery across the road."

"It's not funny, Anto'. I've been seriously thinking about it."

"Married men have affairs when they hit middle age... and you - "

"Celibacy... that's what I need. Or a good woman."

Antonio hands him the pick-up slip. "They'll be ready on Thursday. But tell me, what keeps you from getting a good woman?"

"I'm rusty, I guess. Don't know how to go about it anymore. Of course, if someone could put in a good word for me, things might be different."

"Sounds like you have your eyes on someone already."

"I sure do," he laughs. "And come to think of it, you're the one who could help me out. You know *Lucia...?* Your cousin Lucia – Donatelli?"

"Yeah, I know my cousin Lucia Donatelli," Antonio says, somewhat touchy. "What of it? You're not thinking of courting *her?*"

"Why not? She's attractive... and sharp. I could go for her no problem."

"You could, could you?" says Antonio, grinding stones with his teeth.

"Very much so."

Antonio turns around, to see where his wife is. Then seeing that she's way at the back, busy at the ironing board, he suddenly let's himself go into a fury. He grabs Giovanni by the front of his shirt and shakes him back and forth. "You put one of your dirty paws on Lucia Donatelli and you're dead meat!"

"Christ," says Giovanni, as he shakes himself loose. "I am not a dog. Besides, I don't know what you're getting all riled up about. After all, she's not even your *first* cousin!" He has never seen Antonio react this way over anything before, and certainly has never known him to be deep into all that *respect* and *honour* stuff, either. So what gives with the man, Giovanni wonders?

He's almost home when suddenly something makes him swing his sports car around. Squealing tires, Giovanni heads for the cleaners again.

He slaps at the bell sitting beside the cash register, demanding attention.

Antonio sees him, but takes his merry time coming to the front.

"More dirty clothes?" he laughs.

"No. No dirty clothes this time."

"Forget something then?"

"Yes, that I did."

"And what may that be, my friend?"

"I forgot to *think*. That's what I forgot. But now I got it all figured out."

"And what did you figure out?"

"What I figured out, you say? I will tell you what I figured out! I saw how many times you came around to her place this winter... always carrying your little tool box - to make it look like you were going to fix her pipes. So you're the dog, after all... you're the dirty dog..."

Antonio looks back, toward the ironing board and his wife.

"Don't worry," says Giovanni. "For now you're safe... your trusting wife is wearing earplugs. But don't forget, she only wears them here, inside the cleaners, not out there where people *talk*. And you watch and see, sooner or later, she'll find out about you and Lucia."

"Look, you good for nothing. One word of this to anyone and I'll kill you!"

"*Vaffanculo!*" says Giovanni, dragging out the word nice and slow. "You're worth shit like me." Then he throws some fifty dollar bills on the counter and tells Antonio to see that his clothes get delivered back to him as soon as possible.

"Wait!" says the man, becoming somewhat humble. "This is too much."

"Keep the change. You might need it when your wife throws you out on the street, empty pockets and all."

It's just as well they'd never really been friends, Giovanni thinks, as he walks out of Antonio's Dry Cleaners, to never go back as long as he lives. At home, he opens a bottle of beer and takes a long swallow. Then, standing at the kitchen window, he watches Lucia's white sheets, blowing in the wind.

Abandoned Wedding Ring

Her right arm must have been asleep, for now she's feeling that sudden electric current of awakening flesh, zapping her from elbow to wrist, hand. The blind burning of her fingertips will not let her release the corner of the fitted sheet, which the mattress must have yielded to the force of her restlessness sometime through the night.

Soon, her brain awakens to better clarity, and automatically her left hand reaches for the pillow next to her. Slowly, Elena pulls it close, then moves her head a little, enough to allow for better breathing, subtle inhaling...

It's all still there, the smell of him. Absorbed into the invisible pores of the pillow's foam, the threads of the two layers of cotton cloth encasing it. It's all still there, that smell, that if she were to wash the pillow, it could never be simulated, nor found again. Not even in its smallest intimation, no matter how keen or sharp one's senses were. A mélange of Drakkar Noir cologne and after shave... the sharp peppery breath, washed over by whiffs of cool mint... traces from the odd squirt of L'Oreal hair spray... pungent sweat and sweet camomille soap... and something that could be tangible - if one were to measure and compare its substance to that of the more illusive scents - but at the same time is not. Not when it's made up of mere specks, which could only be observed under a microscope: the thin, invisible peelings of time discarded flesh - normal shedding of the human body.

How often do human beings replace their skin, she wonders?

And how much of his skin did Dario leave behind in the large bed that is no longer considered matrimonial property - or should it be *possession*? Not much, she guesses. How many men would leave a thoughtful and considerate parting gift for their wives, after deciding to put an end to their marriage? Still, she wishes there had been a greater molting; big flakes she could brush into a little pile at the edge of the bed, and let fall into the palm of her hand, for further arranging and safekeeping.

And then what? Would she store the dead bits of skin in the freezer the way she stores her Italian flavoured bread crumbs...?

But no, wait. Better still; some widows keep the ashes of their beloved and departed husbands in delicate urns, proudly displayed on the mantle. She could pretend to be a widow, couldn't she?

Oh God, she had better pull her mind back, harness her thoughts. She knows it's no good to let one's· mind slip into strange realms, in such a seemingly harmless way. It's the things that seem harmless which usually end up being pretty serious. A harmless flirtation... a harmless lie... a harmless extramarital affair...All those harmless things that some people go on doing throughout their lives with bland sophistication, bravery almost.

But Elena is not brave at all in that respect. Has never been. And to her, crazy thoughts spell out trouble. Insanity scares her. And so it should - she has to be *aware*. She has to *know* the dangers. That, of course, brings her back to Dario's pillow. What to do with it?

Suddenly, there are tears in her eyes. They have come un-
bidden, without the preamble of any strong emotion. They're just
there to wash over her eyes, to sponge her cheeks... rinse away
the last residue of anger, pain, resentment.

She lets herself cry for a long time, perhaps even longer than
she's allowed herself before. But even with all that cleansing, she
knows she can't part with the pillow yet; she can't bring herself
to accept termination. She has to devise something. Just for a little while longer. A little while longer.

And so she thinks of a glass case. Preserve the pillow in a
glass case, the way the church preserves the relics of dead saints.
But what good would that do? She couldn't get to it anymore; it
would be sealed away. How could she bring that desperately
longed for smell to her nostrils ever again? Would she not want
to smash the case, shatter the glass and take the pillow out, in her
frantic need to evoke... *evoke what?* There's nothing in her life
with Dario that she wants to bring back.

Yet, why does she still wake up every morning to this small
aberration? Why the compulsive little whiffs? Better still, why
can't she simply stuff the pillow into a plastic bag, and put it out
on the curb on garbage day?

Yes, she desperately needs to dispose of it. She needs to per-
form this last rite, this benediction on her life.

She also needs to wash the sheets and the blankets, for he's
still there, too, deep in every fibre of the bedding (she used to
change her bed every week, but now it's been a month – she has
purposely left it). She could spray Lysol on the mattress, and let
everything air with the window wide open. There's a list of practical exercises she could carry out, as part of a sensible regimen,
guaranteed to be therapeutic for her condition.

But what exactly is her condition? How can she properly describe it at this point, on this particular morning? A month after the note on the counter, his closet empty and the suitcases gone... the Volvo no longer in the garage. The built-in safe empty of his fine gold chains, his birth certificate, and all other personal documents. His wedding ring abandoned in the drawer of the night table...

Slowly, Elena makes herself get up. She walks over to the bathroom. It's the functions of the body that keep one going, she thinks. Nothing else.

The Blue House

The man opens his eyes and sees the boy. He has come to sit beside him on the bench.

"You were sleeping," says the boy. He's about four or five.

"No ... no ... just resting my eyes."

It's a warm evening and the boy is wearing shorts. He's pudgy and his legs are soft and rosy. The man puts out his hand to touch the tender flesh, but then pulls back.

"My grandfather has a cane, too. But it's not fancy like yours. You must be rich!"

The man laughs.

The boy jams his hands between his knees and aims at his toes.

"Bang - bang," he shouts. "Dead!"

"Do you live around here?" enquires the man.

"Over there," he tells him, pointing a chubby finger straight ahead. There's a small wooded lot between the park and the street. "The blue house."

"Oh. Yes. I see it now - between those branches over there. It's the colour of robins' eggs."

The boy shrugs. "I never saw any robins' eggs. I don't know what they look like."

"I see … And your mother – does she know where you are? Did you tell her where you were going?"

He kicks his legs, first one and then the other. "My sister babysits me at night. But she's always talking on the phone. That's all she ever does. I never tell her anything."

"Well, I could hurt you," says the man after a while. "I could do things to you – I could hurt you."

The boy slides back and forth on the seat. Then suddenly stops, to peer down into the grass. The ground is still soft from the afternoon rain and a worm is starting to work itself out of the earth.

"But I know how to run," he says, as if he has suddenly remembered to answer. He slides off the seat.

The man notices the boy's shoe laces; they have come undone. "You could fall down," he tells him. "That could happen."

But the boy is not listening anymore; he's busy trying to pull the worm out as far as it'll come. "I go fishing sometimes," he murmurs absently. "I have to get my own bait."

"Fishing . . . that's nice," says the man, beginning to sweat. "I used to do that too, when I was young. I used to catch pickerel and trout. Big ones, too." His chest feels tight.

"Jimmy," a young girl calls. They can't see her, but she's not too far away from where they are.

"Jimmy!" she calls again, louder.

"That's her," says the boy, putting his head up for the second time. He doesn't really want to leave the worm alone now that he's almost got it all the way out.

"You little brat. Where are you? Wait till I get you!"

The man feels a pain starting to spread underneath his right shoulder and he quickly reaches into his pocket for the little plastic container. "You'd better go," he murmurs, putting a tiny pill underneath his tongue. "Better – "

"Eh, stupid," the sister hollers again. "Get back here right now!"

Reluctantly dropping the worm, Jimmy gives a deep sigh. "She thinks she can boss me around, but watch and see. When I grow up, I am going to beat her up."

Arms swinging at his sides, he starts to leave.

The man gets up from the bench quickly. "Eh kid ... don't come back," he shouts, gripping his cane so tight his knuckles hurt. "Stay away from this place from now on. Do you hear?"

"Why," says the boy, nonchalantly.

"Never mind - just don't. You don't understand. Anything could happen - anything."

Laughing, the boy turns a somersault. But when he's about to do another one, suddenly he changes his mind. He starts to run home, instead.

Left alone, the man stares for a long time at the blue peak of a house he can barely see through the gently swaying leaves.

The Last
Frozen Dinner

Marco wakes up and sits on the edge of the bed, smiling. His expression is very much like that of a young man perched on a high wall, swinging his legs back and forth, knowing the world is soon going to start blossoming in front of him. The truth is, however, that Marco is fifty-six years old and the smile genetic.

His mother used to say it was in their background... fun loving Scottish Catholics, who had immigrated to Italy during the Reformation, and happy-go-lucky Italians from deep in the Alps.

Just as well he's blessed with a good disposition. One of his ancestors, aspiring to become fully assimilated into the Italian culture, had one day foolishly changed his name from MacDonald to Maccadonaldi, a family name Marco had no choice inheriting...

Strangely, the name had given him no trouble whatsoever while growing up in Italy, but in Canada it's another story. Marco tends to gravitate toward Italian Canadian women, and they all think the name is weird. As soon as he mentions it to them, they look at him funny and proceed to ask, "Maccadonaldi? Are you sure?" as if one could easily make a mistake about his own last name.

He has even come to blame the failure of his relationships - or, to be more exact, the lack of them - on his surname. Well, maybe not totally; he knows better than that. But that's what he used to always tell his mother, knowing perhaps there might even be a grain of truth in it.

The woman had never let a day go by without reminding him it was not a good idea for him to remain a bachelor the rest of his life. Especially when he didn't even have a niece or nephew around to take care of burying him when the time came.

"But what can I do...?" he commiserated with her jokingly, one day last year. It was just before she went on her trip to Italy. "I can't help it if I can't find a wife. Besides, you know how it is... as soon as they hear the word Maccadonaldi, they start laughing. Then, caput, everything is over."

"Well!" she exclaims, tiny body standing straight, erect. "Learn to do like I do. When people make fun of me for something, I laugh along with them. It always works!"

"Ma, porco cane!" he swears in the good-natured manner he has been doing for years. "That's what I do, too. But then they figure that's all I am good for... you know... good for a laugh."

Suddenly, she stops wiping the stove and turns to look at him. *"Figlio...* I always wanted to ask you this... Is everything all right? Is everything the way it should be?"

Frowning, he puts his newspaper down, folds it without looking at it.

"What do you mean by that?"

"You know what I mean."

"No, I don't. What are you talking about?"

"Non comprendi?" she finally asks, her small, dark eyes squinting. "I mean are you okay... are you normal? I know you were born with all the parts a man should have - when you were a baby there

34

was nothing wrong with your *testicole*... and nothing wrong with the other thing either..."

Exasperated, Marco shakes his head and runs his hands through his hair. Should he kill her? She sure deserves it. But what is the use. The woman has never been shy and reserved, and with the years she'll only keep getting worse. He might as well get used to it. Anyway, soon she'll be gone for a month, and that will give him a break from having to listen to her... and her impudent talk.

At the same time, he knows he shouldn't complain. Who else takes care of him the way his mother does? Full of arthritis, the woman has managed to prepare him fifty frozen dinners from scratch: thirty for the month she'll be away... and the other twenty to do him for a while, in case the plane carrying her is going to go down...

• • •

The airport is four hundred miles away, but he doesn't mind driving her there - he would never think of letting his mother take the airbus. She knows they have to leave by one o'clock... but still insists on cooking a meal before going.

"I will not eat in a restaurant," she tells him, as she scurries around the kitchen, a large apron tied firmly around her waist. "I like to know the hands that have prepared my food..."

For the flight, she is taking her own sandwiches and fruit.

"Have it your way, but no need to make a feast, for God's sake. We haven't got that much time. Planes don't wait!"

Marco goes out to the garage to get his car ready: adds oil and washer fluid, cleans the windshield, and wipes the passenger side so his mother won't get her good clothes soiled.

When he goes back inside, he tags her suitcase and locks it. Then he looks in her travel bag, to see if she has all her medications.

Although she never complains, the woman has a dozen ailments.

"Make sure you carry your purse in front of you all the time, when you're over there. Italy is full of robbers!"

Marco worries about her travelling alone. She's such a little woman, they could push her over like a feather.

"Oh, stop worrying," she tells him. "I have gone back to Italy seven times, and nothing has ever happened to me. Worry about yourself."

"And what do I have to worry about," he laughs.

"A lot of things," she sighs. "For one, you can't even turn the oven on."

"I'm sure I'll manage. Besides, there's a whole troop of Italian widows on this street I can call on for help."

"Oh yes," she says, glad to be reminded, "that's just what I was going to tell you… If you need anything while I am gone, the widow Angelucci is the one to call. She's the most sensible of them all… goes out only when she has to… Not like the rest of them, playing bingo all day long!"

"I think I'd be out of luck there, Mamma," he says earnestly. "That woman won't even turn and look at me when I happen to go by. She talks to me only when you're around - out of respect for you, I suppose."

"Oh yes, that's right," she nods with pity. "I forgot about that… how you used to argue with her husband all the time… Here, take your plate to the table… That's too bad, isn't it - about the widow Angelucci, I mean? Especially since she's just the right age for you - turned fifty the other day. And her children all grown up and nicely settled… Really, Marco, I don't know why you always manage to antagonize the best women around…"

"Beats me," he says, just to keep the conversation going - there will be enough time to catch up on silence while she's gone.

She ponders for a moment. "Well, you know what you could do...? You could do what they used to do in some parts of Italy..."

"What's that?"

"Go out with a sack... stick it over a woman's head, and – "

"Eh, that's a possibility," he cuts in quickly, sprinkling cheese on his rigatoni. "But then I would have to go and buy another house. I couldn't bring a woman I just kidnapped to live with her mother-in-law, could I? Abduction is bad enough. Who needs a mother-in-law thrown in, too?"

Sometimes his mother does get under his skin, driving him to sarcastic replies that are not even relevant. Childish defense, really. But they have never apologized to one another for anything, and somehow they always manage to work their way back to friend-liness. They're too fond of each other for anything else. Besides, they just don't know how to hold grudges.

"So, that's it. I am old and I am in the way," she says. "But... as I told you the other day... the planes... there's one falling every day."

"Yes," he laughs, trying to make amends with his usual scathing humour. "But the plane you'll be on is going to make it all the way to Milano, even if the motors burn out... Mamma, believe me, you'll live to be a hundred, just so you can drive your only son crazy."

"No," she says, suddenly wiping tears from her eyes. "No. *Non ritorno.* I will not come back."

"Ah. Stop that."

He hates it when she starts moping. Thank God it doesn't happen very often. *"No, non ritorno,"* she says again, strangely adamant.

Slowly, she begins to clear the table.

•••

That was the last meal they had together. It wasn't the plane, but a heart attack.

It cost Marco a fortune to have his mother buried in Italy. He wanted to bring her body back to Canada, but his aunt talked him out of it. "What's the point?" she told him over the phone. "Most of her loved ones are buried over here... Besides, this is her native soil - her own country..."

It made a lot of sense, and he didn't bother arguing.

Taking a quick flight, he went over to do what needed to be done. Marco gave his mother a proper funeral... bought her a fine marble headstone. He even ordered a perpetual lamp to be installed on her resting-place... a light to shine on her name forever...

Anna Maccadonaldi, nee McAuley.

• • •

He and his mother had always been good to each other, and Marco has no regrets. But sometimes he can't help wondering about the timing of her death. He now feels almost certain that she willed herself to die in Italy, knowing it would be the only sure way she would end up being buried beside her husband, Marco's father, who had died many years ago. She had never spoken to him about her last wishes, but Marco knew his mother well: when she wanted something bad enough, she always found a way to get it!

But damn, he does miss the old woman.

Sometimes, at supper, Marco catches himself lifting his head to talk to her across the table, and she's not there. Then he goes and puts music on, sings along with Pavarotti and Bocelli... When the song Pagliaccio comes on, he turns the stereo off, afraid of the tears that might pop into his eyes...

He fights sadness like hell: it's something that has been bred in him.

His mother's frozen dinners are all gone, except one: the last one. He just couldn't bring himself to eat it. It has now been in the freezer for six months and it's probably no good anymore. He knows he has to throw it out, but he doesn't have the heart to do it.

His own cooking has no resemblance to the delicious meals his mother used to make. He just has no patience with pots and pans. He has made pasta with tomato sauce that smelled of burnt so bad that even a dog would have turned his nose from it.

"La vita è proprio una fregatura," he sighs. "Life is truly a rip-off."

Suddenly, Marco rubs his face and gets off the edge of the bed. How long has he been sitting there, remembering? Too long. He picks up his jeans from the floor and puts them on. Slowly, he walks to the window...

The blinds are closed and he lifts a couple of slats to peek outside. The snowstorm the weatherman has been predicting for two days has finally arrived. Marco, who works in construction, is glad he hasn't been asked to do overtime this weekend. For two days, if he wants to, he can stay in the house nice and warm!

Across the street, the widow Angelucci is busy shoveling snow in her driveway. She has boots up to her knees, and a wool hat that comes down to her nose... men's rubber gloves on her hands. Thin as a rake, but God can she shovel!

He wonders what she eats for supper... or lunch for that matter. Does she eat at all?

Marco goes back to his bed and searches for his shirt. Where the hell did he put it last night? Finally finds it, tangled up with his blankets. He has to learn to be more organized - neatness is not one of his virtues... and one of these days he should clean the house, too. It's starting to look like a dump!

But he has never used a vacuum cleaner in his life, never washed a floor. Where would he begin? He would rather dig a ditch any day!

The widow Angelucci must do a lot of cleaning. One day last week, he found himself behind her at the checkout counter of the local grocery store and, for a moment, he couldn't help looking at her hands.

They were so red... raw, almost ready to bleed.

Still, he might have liked to touch those hands... rough as they were..."

"Ah, forget it," he tells himself, as he puts his slippers on. "What you need, Marco Maccadonaldi, is a nice cup of espresso with grappa... Anyway, she's too skinny. What's there to grab with a woman like that?"

But when he's at the bottom of the stairs, suddenly, an impulse overtakes him... and instead of heading for the kitchen, Marco goes straight to the back door. Quickly, he slips his parka on, searches for warm gloves...

Shovel over his shoulder, he crosses the road.

"*Buongiorno, Signora* Angelucci," he greets cheerfully, as he reaches her sidewalk. "Looks like winter is finally here." And he digs in with his shovel on the other side of her driveway, where the wind has made a tall drift.

The woman pushes roughly at her hat, to find her eyes. "What are you doing?" she demands. "Go and shovel your own driveway. My Giovanni would never have wanted you to set foot on our property..."

He's just about to answer and say, "Your Giovanni was nothing but a troublemaker... always arguing with everyone. If it wasn't the fence, it was a cat or a dog... or some other damn thing touching his balls the wrong way..." but luckily, caution put a quick bite on Marco's tongue before the stream of words had a chance to come out.

"Oh, I know. I know," he finally manages to say in a soothing tone. "You have every right to feel the way you do... But, you see, *Signora*, I never meant to interfere. It was the neighbours... they were the ones who came to me for help... They thought, since I was Italian too, I would be a good mediator over their arguments with your husband..."

"You Italian?" she snorts. "That's a good one!"

"What do you mean by that?"

"Don't you think I know? You're *scozzese*."

"Oh. So now I am not even Italian anymore," he laughs. "What kind of talk is that? You were friends with my mother ... you don't think she was Italian? Didn't she speak and cook Italian? Didn't she do everything Italian? If you ask me, there was no woman around more Italian than my mother..."

"Well, I didn't ask you."

"Okay, let's talk about my father, then. That man never knew any other country but Italy. In fact, neither did his father and his grandfather – and even his great grandfather, for that matter."

"What about the blood...?"

"The blood? Well... the blood... Sure, there's some Scottish blood in my background, but only God knows how many generations ago. Anyway, what difference does it make?"

"Well... Giovanni told me once that if you ever got married, you'd wear a skirt for the wedding."

"You mean a kilt?"

"Isn't that the same thing?"

"What are you trying to say?"

"A skirt is a skirt."

Yes. And screw you, too, *femmina*, he thinks.

But he can't let her get away with a comment like that; some things are just not in his nature.

"Look, *Signora* Angelucci," he starts out all sweet and mellow.

"I've had women pick on my last name... but never have I come across one who made fun of me about kilts. And you're not even that good looking!"

He can't see her face; it's hidden between hat and scarf... but there is no pause in her movement, no pause at all. She's one sure woman!

Heads bent, they both keep the snow flying.

He finishes with the left side of the driveway and goes to help her on the right, starting at the opposite end. And then, there they are, face to face, breathing cold smoke toward each other...

Finally, she speaks.

"I made *ciambelle* last night," she says, loosening her scarf, peeling off her hat. "The kind your mother used to make..."

Ah, now we're talking, he thinks.

"Sweet bagels are good only when they're fresh..."

"Yes, I remember..."

Up close, Lucia Angelucci is a pretty woman. Her brown eyes are soft, warm... her smile youthful.

He looks at her for a minute... she looks back at him and laughs.

A big grin cracking open the frozen skin of his cheeks, Marco sets his shovel against the corner of her house and follows her inside.

Snow on the Roofs

After knocking on her door, he walks back to the edge of the veranda to wait. His shoulder twitches. Tension begins to build up on the left side of his face.

She doesn't ask him to sit down, but he knows it's all right. There are only two chairs, one on each side of the small, narrow table. The baby chair is in the corner. She has forgotten to wipe it clean; spills of baby food have dried on its tray. He thinks he can smell peaches.

"I'm late. I was away in Europe for three weeks…"

"Doesn't matter." She doesn't smile, but her voice is mild.

She fills him a cup with coffee, herself taking a mug. She knows he's not fond of mugs.

He leans toward the cup. "It's a dreary night. The snow… too heavy on the roofs."

She seals her mug with the palm of her hand - a strange habit. The warmth of the coffee is felt by her cheeks.

She never asks him if he wants to see the child - she knows

he doesn't come for that. From the beginning, it was settled. Still, he likes to enquire politely about his health.

"He had impetigo... but he's better now."

"A virus?" It's been so long, he can't remember – he's a grand-father now.

"Yes – virus."

"But he's really better now, you say?"

"Yes, don't worry." She has a way of letting her gaze fall away from his eyes and attaching it to some other object nearby. The dark eyes won't budge after that.

She never offers a second cup of coffee and he feels he has to go. He gets up and pushes his chair forward, aligning it care-fully with the table. "It's time," he murmurs. "It's getting late."

"There's another storm – the radio said."

"It held for a while."

She's attracted to the window, stands there staring into the blizzard. He runs his fingers over the front of his coat, and find-ing it still buttoned, lets his other hand dip into his pocket. He places the envelope beside his empty cup, pushing it under the saucer a bit.

"Some people won't get home tonight..." He has spoken a bit too loud.

Startled, she holds her pulse tight, before turning his way.

"She'll worry about you – your wife."

"Yes."

He circles his scarf around his neck. "Good night."

He tries to find his way to the subway. It isn't easy. The wind whistles in his ears... snow twirls all around him.

Blueberry Muffins

I can see she is going to pass my demo table in a hurry, until she catches sight of the blueberry muffins baking in my convection oven. She stops her shopping cart and grins, teeth missing on the upper left of her mouth.

"Blueberries, is it, dear?"

"Yes," I smile, eager to make my sales pitch. "Blueberry muffins. I'll have samples ready for you to try in ten minutes - they're more than half done... I am promoting our non-stick bake ware. It's silicone coated and you don't have to grease or pray." I turn to show her the wide selection on the long table behind me.

"We have twenty-five percent off everything here."

"Twenty-five percent, eh?"

"Yes," I nod, putting on my oven mitt to turn the muffin tin around. I am having trouble with the little oven not baking evenly.

"My! They look good. I used to make them muffins for my son all the time... Gary, that's his name. He's twenty-six now. Went to university four years - he did. Used to come home so hungry all the time. But he's working now.

"He's with Lambert's. They're a franchise - all over Ontario. Gary is in Windsor, that's where he is. Of course, there's not as much money in sales as there is in business. That's where he wants to be in the future - business. But this'll give him experience. They made him manager right away - assistant. They're training him.

"He comes home every Saturday night. He used to eat so much before, but now all he wants is soup and a sub. Mom, he says, that's all I want and I'll be fine.

"My husband, he's in drafting. Of course, he hasn't been able to get much work lately. Hardly worked at all last year. Then he had six weeks. Six good weeks, mind you. We caught up on all our payments, we did. He makes very good money when he works. He does! And we paid back everything. Oh, we did. Went and left ourselves with only one pay cheque. Of course, that wasn't too smart. It didn't go very far. We should have kept more... He's been promised a job in Toronto. This engineer he knows, he's already picked him to do the drawings. They just have to wait for the go ahead on the job. It could be a while yet. Not too long, though... How are they coming? Starting to look golden, them blueberry muffins..."

"Yes, getting there," I say, smoothing the front of my white smock. "I have to make sure they're done in the middle."

"We used to live good once. Oh, we sure did enjoy ourselves. Travelled all over, we did. Went everywhere... Las Vegas, Jamaica. Of course, when my husband worked out of town, I always went along with him. Those days were great. We went to nightclubs all the time, and saw a lot of big stars. We saw Frank Sinatra, and Elvis, too. We did everything in those days... Don't burn them now. You wouldn't want to do that."

"Just two more minutes. That's all," I say. "The timer will go off."

"Did you know you can buy liver for 59 cents a pound? Yes, we buy it all the time. It's good, too! And chicken, now that's not too expensive if you pick it up on special. You just have to know where to shop. I buy apples all the time, though. You need fruit. Can't go without it... There was a time when I used to buy so much extra, but now we make menus. Monday and Saturday, we have liver – oh, we do like liver. Chicken twice a week... potatoes with it. Fish one night. If you know what kind to buy, fish's not dear at all. Then we have a treat once in a while. A person needs a treat. Just some little thing to leave one a bit satisfied."

I take the muffins out of the oven. Placing a few of them on a cutting board, I begin to make small portions to set out on the serving plate for store customers to sample.

"Help yourself, ma'am. Go ahead."

"Oh yes, yes."

But before picking up her sample, she leans over to look into a small bowl I have on the side. "Is that butter in there, dear? I'd like butter on it. Muffins aren't the same without butter. Lots of it, please."

"So many people have to watch their weight... or their cholesterol," I explain. "That's why I don't put butter on them... but we always have it handy. Well, here we are," I smile.

Slowly, she pushes her cart forward. "Blueberries are always just right – not too sweet. I like blueberries." Then glancing at her watch, she backs up a few steps. "My husband will have supper ready when I get back. Just in time. Chicken. He cooks it just right. Could I have another piece? My husband would love a piece, dear..."

At first I am not sure, but then I know what to do. I cut open a whole muffin and fill it with the soft butter. I hand it to her on a napkin.

Her eyes gleam. "That's nice. Bless your heart... yes..."

She turns into the next aisle. More customers come up and I don't have time to think about the woman anymore. But when I notice her leaving the store without any groceries, I can't help wondering for a second if she will have any supper tonight.

A Little Visiting

She's the oldest Italian woman he knows and he thinks about her a lot. Well, perhaps not the oldest, the oldest who hasn't gone senile. He remembers her smile. A quick grin, sly with arrogance.

"What a bad girl you are," people tease her, for she has no shame when it comes to making a pun. And she sure has one up her sleeve every time. Beppa is always happy. Always fascinated by something or other. Her only complaint in life is about her thin, thin legs that play unbecoming tricks on her stockings. She says she doesn't mind the wrinkles on her neck, even though she plays at rubbing them away with her bony fingers all the time. Her face doesn't reveal her age, a flat kind of face and brown.

This makes him think of pancakes, Canadian food he's watched his grandchildren breakfast on. When they were little and he younger, he'd refuse to eat the things. "Try them, Nonno," they'd entice, making yummy with their lips. But he would laugh and wrinkle his nose in dislike of them. Then one morning not long ago, Anna had placed a plate with them in front of him, and when he looked at her questioningly, she disregarded him, maybe her mind on other things. Slowly he began to eat them.

He'd not wanted to make any fuss, for he cared for Anna, wished he could do something to take away her sadness. Over the last ten yeas she'd opened the door and watched her four children leave, like migrating birds, going now south, now north, returning to their home nest only for brief visits between moving trips. But that isn't what makes her sad; Anna's glad her children have turned out so well, are doing fine with their own families. It's really that she'd not expected to lose Domenic, a man who never had to take a pill - not even for a headache - all his life.

His only son that son was. He misses him every day. Yet... even though it is perhaps a sin, he finds it natural to have been the one to do the burying.

His life seems to be starting over. An easy and kindly life. Newsmen on TV and younger people he knows talk about all the horrors and atrocities in the world, and sometimes close to home, but he can't envision any of it. The link is not there anymore; too many years have stretched between the days of his sacrifices and hardships and his present worry-free existence.

So many years that his wife's face, rest her soul, he can't even recall, except the dark sheen of her hair when he'd first met her, her perpetual frown... a blue-veined hand counting beads on a chestnut-coloured rosary. And even those frail recollections come to him only when his daughters are there to aid his memory with their strong inheritance of maternal features.

Trieste and Luisa are good to him. But he's a little shy of them. They married young and he's never really gotten close to them - not the way he has with Anna.

After the wedding, Anna came to live in the big house he and Domenic had bought and fixed up, and she'd felt at home from the very start. And now at times he even forgets that she's not his own flesh and blood.

She's been looking awfully tired lately and she's made an unusual number of trips to the doctor and he's worried about her. He doesn't think it proper to prod and ask - he doesn't wish to embarrass her - her ailment could be due to menopause. He hopes it's nothing worse.

He wonders if something were to happen to her which one of his daughters would take him in. He'd rather it be Trieste. He has heard - when he wasn't supposed to - that she has a lover... and when her Marco is full of wine, she let's his friend Armando slip in from the back door. Serves that donkey right. A drink or two is needed, but the fifth takes away a man's rights. Trieste is the one who's always singing and never complains about her husband's behaviour - a sure sign that she's not waiting for Marco to sober up so she can have some fun.

He laughs to himself and thinks: It would be interesting to be part of that household... to pass away the time guessing if Marco or Armando had been the one to put the twinkle in Trieste's eyes the night before.

Beppa's eyes twinkle too. Small in their shrunken pouches. Little stars of eyes.

Beppa beats him in age by three years; she's ninety-eight. She beats him at everything. At walking for sure; he's done with that. Or maybe his legs have become lazy since Anna bought him that nice tricycle.

He shuffles to the closet in the front hall to get his coat. Always has to search for it way back - Anna's doing. She tries to keep it from his reach so that he'll wear one of the newer ones at hand. But he likes the old one. Anna, who is not really a nagger, says its lambs-wool collar looks chewed up by some hungry little animal. But he feels comfortable in it; it's the right length for shifting his legs on his vehicle, and not too heavy on his shoulders if the weather unexpectedly warms up.

"When you come back we'll make sausages," says Anna.

He wants to tell her that there's no need. He can't eat sausages like hefty Domenic would, like her sturdy sons. He's an old man. The last sausages they made ended up feeding the neighbour-hood's German shepherd. But he doesn't remind her; she can af-ford the waste – she's been left well provided. "All right, Anna, we'll make sausages," he assents.

He mounts his tricycle. This will likely be his last ride before the treacherous winter cold, for the season has already begun on the calendar. The extra offering of autumn has been good. He's never been fond of winter and with the years it has become a true obstacle.

He shouldn't even go out today: it's impending weather. It'll snow or rain, or both. But he doesn't feel weaned yet for the long months of stale air in the house. He thinks of sunny days... of lilacs and perfume in the air... tulip patches and the velvet of marigolds... He sees the children on the swings in the neigh-bourhood park... hears the shrieks of joy as their limbs point to the sky... And there are the young mothers who take time to smile at him as he sits there, bemused at the liveliness that he's somehow part of and yet excluded from.

Today he heads for the new subdivision still under con-struction. One S-shaped street. He likes to go there; the men all wave at him. The self-employed ones, who don't have to worry about stopping their work, even come out to the curb to talk to him. They call him Fillippo Antico... ancient Filippo. That is nice.

This time it's Aldo who comes to greet him. He's beaming "new-father" all over. He tells him about his new baby girl so ex-citedly that all Filippo can make out from the rush of words is that the baby has more hair than he, the papa, ever had. He con-gratulates him with a firm handshake, and then tells him an old-country joke appropriate to the over-excited state of a new father. Aldo laughs until his eyes cry. He is still laughing when he goes back to his work, of mortar and bricks. Filippo watches as the young man repeats the joke to his partner brother, who also laughs. Another man shakes his head in wonder and marvels at Filippo's undying wit and zest.

He pedals on, slowly. He likes to observe everything. And as he does that, he begins to feel a yearning to be working with these men. He feels melancholic because once, as a carpenter, he'd been part of such construction teams. He can hear the thump, thump of his heart. He recalls the camaraderie... the daily satisfaction of earning for himself and his family. "Work of the hands... it is fine work," he hears himself murmur.

By the time he finishes his leisurely round and gives one last wave of the hand to a group of labourers and tradesmen, his longing has been replaced by a feeling of contentment... for he's reasoned with himself and knows that in his life he's been truly blessed... and this is all a plus, the men giving him a bit of their world to carry home - to keep and store away - to savour at his mind's command during the hibernating months ahead.

"They're good men," he affirms along the way, as though he knew each one of them as he knows himself.

And he's really glad he can give them something back for the good feeling they provide for him. For the younger fellows he's never short of a bit of a tale or a joke to lighten up their day. For the older ones, he automatically offers proof that life can go on for many years after retirement. And he's proof to one and all that a long life does not necessarily mean hospitals, wheelchairs, and bedpans. Life, even though at a slower pace, can be quite rewarding with its small pleasures. Look at how many times he's overheard them say, "By God, think of Filippo *Antico*, maybe we'll reach his age too – be as healthy. Never know!" He's more than their horseshoe for luck... he's their living augury. He's the foreteller of hopes rendered.

On his way home, he abandons his usual route so he can pass in front of the house where Beppa lives. He hasn't seen her to talk to in months. But of course he's being silly; she wouldn't be outside today – there's no work to be done in her daughter's garden or yard, now. Three weeks ago he'd seen her stuffing the last of the fallen leaves in plastic bags and he'd waved at her from Anna's car. "Quite the girl," Anna had remarked. And he had smiled to himself remembering what he'd been told by Beppa's son-in-law... how when the old lady had gone on that three week vacation south, with her rich son from Boston, she'd taken a real fancy to gambling. He'd taken her to a plush casino just to let her see the inside of one for the first time but she cared nothing about viewing it – it was the wheel of fortune that got her all excited.

No. Not now nor ever can he imagine that old devil giving up something as vital as breathing. He knows she'll be there at the cemetery, smugly casting her handful of earth onto his grave... more pleased than ever for having outlived him.

He doesn't see her outside and he follows straight home. Back to play harmless and helpless games with gentle-suffering Anna.

In the kitchen he unfolds a large apron and ties it on. And as he helps Anna stuff the chopped meats into the casings, he feels a rise of anger. But toward what? whom? There's nothing he can do. He reminds himself how fortunate he is to be alive at his age... how grateful he must be for being cared for so lovingly. But the anger doesn't leave. A paralyzed kind of anger that cannot be released.

Yes, what can he do. If he would dare knock on her door... if he telephoned to speak to her... Should he? No! he shouldn't even think of it in the remotest way. Gossip about him and Beppa would spread like fire on a dry wheat field. Eyebrows would go up in ultimate wonder at two such old people. There would be laughter over imagined lewdness - he knows the vivid and exaggerated imagination of his people. Honourable intentions always the last to be perceived in one's actions. "That's the curse of the Italians," he almost says aloud, with Anna right across from him.

He wants to cry. He isn't asking for much; only a bit of time together with her so that they can recount things remembered, talk about things forgotten... a few companionable moments with a soul who's lived as many decades as he has.

"You know who I saw in the store yesterday," says Anna, "I saw Rosa. Poor thing has lost so much weight... she told me Carlo has to have the leg amputated."

Sadly Filippo shakes his head. "A good man. Full of respect, too. There was never a Christmas that he didn't come by to give me his good wishes."

"Not this year, Papa. You'll have to go see him... I'll take you - we'll go."

"We used to go everywhere when Domenic was alive," he says suddenly.

Anna takes a deep breath. "We must start again - I know. My doctor won't let me have any more pills and he's right. He says I should start to get out again... make my own life... I suppose a little visiting would be good for a start. I can't face the card parties and dinners yet."

Then she turns to him scared. "You'll go with me sure, won't you? I can't do it on my own, yet."

"Oh, Anna."

The only tears he wants to cry now are big festive ones. He wants to let her know how much he's been waiting for this to happen, but he can't because of the selfish reason behind it. He knows that one of the families they'll be visiting is Beppa's family and he feels happiness spread through him, warm and satisfying. He doesn't know when they'll be going but that doesn't matter. Just knowing that they will is more than sufficient.

He feels so invigorated that he wants to get up and make his feet learn to waltz again... he wants to glide and float by himself... but all he does is smile up at Anna; a smile large enough to encourage anyone to action, small enough to make him restrain his intimate feelings. So, carefully he prepares to tell her: *Yes, a little visiting will be good for both of us.* But instead he hears himself say in a voice that could have belonged to a man still full of youth: "Eh, let's fry up some sausages."

She becomes silent, absent. (Must be what he said.)

"Remember," he urges, "remember the time that after making sausages we cooked so many of them... there was hardly any of them left to hang in the cellar."

"Yes. Big fry-pan on the stove and the electric one full blast."

"And you said we'd be all sick the next day."

"That was the time we all had a bit too much to drink... and the kids learned to drink wine – we felt great the next day." And she laughs.

He's startled. He had forgotten the sound of her girlish laughter. It warms him up and down with joy.

She moves neatly about the kitchen and he can see how the mourning is beginning to shed from her features, reminding him what an attractive woman his son had for a wife.

Suddenly she's in front of his chair; she peers down at him, concern shadowing her soft brown eyes. "What's the matter, Papa? You look so flushed... and there's sweat on your forehead. I hope you're not coming down with the flu – it's going around again."

"Oh, no," he hastens to say. "I feel fine, Anna. Just fine. Maybe a bit tired - it's past my naptime." And he rises.

"I shouldn't have kept you here helping me... but the sausages - did you really want to eat them now?"

"I do... but pork meat - what do you think?"

"Maybe not this late in the day, Papa. Too hard to digest. Tomorrow for lunch, all right?"

"Yes," he says. "Tomorrow."

He pads off to his room. His heart sends Anna many blessings for being resolute in her struggle to adjust to widowhood - it's that which has brought about the wonderful and unexpected advent of events.

Today he even puts on his pajamas so he'll get the best rest. Anything to keep strong and healthy. And he knows that when his head is settled on the soft pillow, he'll even dream a little. No big dreams - something that will not disgrace - something gentle... befitting a man nearing a century of proper living.

Before the Roses Fade

After kissing her baby good night over the crib, Leda lifted her long black hair back onto her shoulders. Sam put his arms around her waist. "Not bad looking our *bambina*," he grinned. "Someday she'll be a beauty queen!" Leda laughed and adjusted his tie. He was a plain fellow, in looks and manner, but she loved him. Everything was perfect.

He went to pick up the babysitter. She wrapped the gift, and wrote a few words on the card, signed it.

The traffic was heavy and they were almost late arriving at the club. A young man in a gray tuxedo hurriedly ushered them to their place, not far from the head table. It was a multi-course dinner... veal, quail, fancy sherbet, exotic fruits. Politicians and dignitaries were present.

Soon the band began to play for the old couple to dance. People stood up and applauded. The old woman had forgotten the steps of the slow tango... she was a lifeless bulk, burdened by a long black dress, covered with sequins. Her agile partner was gentle with her, but after a few turns, tactfully led her back to their place of honour, behind the huge cake, decorated in gold.

"Poor soul," Leda murmured absently.

Shortly after, Sam noticed his wife's nervousness and got her up to dance so that they could talk without being overheard by the other people at their table. "What is going on?" he asked. "Why are people staring at us?"

"Tony... their son," she whispered, "he never stopped looking at me all through dinner. Didn't you notice?"

"Oh, is that all?" he laughed. "I guess I'm getting used to people looking at you. You're the most beautiful woman here tonight."

"Sammy, it's not funny."

Frowning, he pulled her closer. "I know. But don't make anything of it... pretend nothing happened."

"I don't understand. Anyway, why don't we get out of here, Sammy. I don't feel comfortable staying."

He didn't say anything until they were into the next dance. "We can't do that. We can't leave yet... it would be an offence... You haven't lived here very long, so you don't *know*. These people... they're the ones with the money behind the company I work for... and just about every other business around here. They own this city, Leda. Nobody ever slights the Argentini family."

"What are you trying to tell me?"

The lights dimmed. They danced on. Out of the corner of her eyes she saw several men going up to the old man and kissing his hand. The son stood at his father's side, at ease with the ritual.

Tony Argentini rarely smiled, Leda noticed. He was tall, with dark features and smooth black hair that was beginning to go thin at the front. He was in law school, and people said he was brilliant.

Dancing past the head table, she felt dizzy for a moment. Sam quickly supported her. "Damn," he said, not to her.

"It's all right. Just too much dancing. Let's go back to our table."

At eleven o'clock they got up and went to bid their hosts good-bye.

"So soon?" murmured the old man.

"Our babysitter is young and we have to get her home by twelve," Sam explained. "We really must go, Mr. Argentini."

He nodded, and spoke again, in his soft murmuring voice. "It was good of you to come, Sammy Malito. Eh... you played with my sister's kids when you were little, remember? Nice boy... nice."

Removed to the back, between her husband and her son, Mrs. Argentini was sprawled on a chair, fat ankles crossed. She had fallen asleep.

"I heard you have a little daughter," said the son, his dark eyes staring into Leda's. "Best wishes, *Signora...*" Then he bowed and kissed her hand.

As soon as they were outside, Sam took out a cigarette. Lighting it, his hands were shaking so badly he had to use two matches. "The bastard. He pretended I wasn't even there. The bastard."

"Sammy," she said, resting her hand on his knee as he drove, "let's just forget about tonight, pretend it never happened. Let's just think about us... and our beautiful little girl. Don't you think she's perfect? We're so lucky!"

"I know," he said, looking at her. "I think about her all the time. And how can I not think about her, my own flesh and blood? Leda, promise me you'll never let anything happen to our child..."

"Now what kind of talk is that, Sam?"

"Crazy talk. But Leda, you have no idea the things that are going through my mind right now. I know things that you don't..."

"Like what, Sam?"

He took a deep breath. "It goes back many years... My father had a business... a bakery - a legitimate business. Then those damn people came to town - the Argentini. They came from only God knows where... Anyway, Papa was a proud man, stubborn. They wanted him to do things that weren't right, but he wouldn't. He never gave in to them. Never. My mother kept a black dress in her closet all the time... and we all knew why."

"Oh Sam. But why didn't you mention any of this before?"

He didn't answer right away. "It's not something you go around talking about, Leda, and because you can't talk about it, you pretend to forget."

She thought for a moment. "But - nothing did happen to your father, did it?"

"Yeah, that's the ironic part," he said, finally, as they were turning into their driveway. "Papa died of old age."

"Well, you see, Sammy... you're just letting your mind get ahead of you, that's all."

He started to open the car door, but then paused to smile at her for a second. "Maybe you're right, Leda. Maybe you're right."

But later, when he came back from driving the babysitter home, he went straight to the cupboard and poured himself a drink. Then for a long time he stared at his empty glass. "Leda," he said at last. "I think I was being followed."

She reproached him too quickly. "Oh darling, it's so easy to get paranoid about things like this. Please forget it."

But neither one of them *could* forget it, and that night the sheets in their bed remained cold. Their silence had begun... almost a detachment from each other. Each filled with a terrible fear of something vague and horrible happening.

The next day was Sunday and for the first time since they were married, they didn't go to Mass. Dinner remained half uneaten on the table and, later, Leda played with Tania more than usual, exciting the child too much. Sam listened to opera all day.

She hated opera, it always made her head throb. Finally, around nine o'clock, the stereo went silent, and shortly after Sam fell asleep on the couch.

"Thank God," Leda murmured, her fingers digging into her temples.

Hurriedly she put the dishwasher on and finished cleaning the kitchen. Then after watching her baby sleep for a minute, she took two aspirins and went to bed.

Around one in the morning, she suddenly woke up and realized that her husband was not in bed yet. Quickly, Leda turned the light on, slipped into her robe and went downstairs to check.

She found him where she had left him. Strange, though, he had not moved at all. His arm was still hanging at the edge of the couch, the hand flat on the floor. Something was wrong!

Leda's heart began to pound, and panic came over her. She started to shake him and call his name. "Sam - Sammy... Wake up! Sam!"

He lifted his head and glared at her. "Christ! What the hell... what the fuck do you want?"

Trembling, she began to back away - he had never talked to her like that before. "Sorry... I thought... didn't know - sorry."

The following evening, as Leda was searching for a pair of gloves in the hallway closet, she suddenly discovered a bottle of brandy hidden on the shelf, between some old sweaters. The bottle was nearly empty.

"Oh dear Lord, what is happening? What is going on?" she murmured.

Sam came up behind her. Angry, he snatched the bottle from her hand. "Shut up, Leda," he said. "Right now shut up - don't you dare say a word."

The baby whimpered in the other room, and Leda hurried to pick her up. "Oh my angel," she murmured, smothering the child with kisses. "Angel."

After that, Sam didn't seem to care anymore if Leda knew he was drinking or not. At night he always went to bed drunk, and in the morning, he poured brandy in his coffee until his mug was too full.

Leda's nerves got so bad that she could scarcely go out anymore… and when the phone rang she jumped, even if her husband was home safe and sound, the baby tightly snuggled in her arms.

● ● ●

Leda had lost over thirty pounds when it happened. Sam was a wisp of a man in his coffin…

He had been well liked in the town and a lot of people came to pay their respects. There was a long line going up to his casket.

Friends lightly kissed Leda on both cheeks… acquaintances held her hands for a long time.

People whispered among themselves: "So tragic. No safety on construction. No safety at all."

For three weeks her mother came to take care of little Tania. Then one day the woman put on her coat and caressed Leda's hair. "The child is your responsibility," she said, anguished. "The time has come for me to leave."

Slowly, Leda started doing her chores again. She hugged her daughter when she had to… and soon tenderness opened up her heart again.

One morning, a few weeks later, the doorbell rang. It was the florist. Leda took the long box to the table and slowly opened it. She counted twelve red roses. The enclosed card read: *Belated condolences… Tony Argentini.*

In Tania's room, she leaned over the crib and looked at her sleeping child for a long time. She picked up the tiny hand… so light and plump, warm. Two tears fell from Leda's eyes and rolled onto the child's white blanket. She would have to put the roses in a vase before they faded.

A Place I
Once Knew

The church stands across from the river. Further down, you can see a factory with tall stacks. We're attending a special celebration, the church's 75th anniversary. When Mass is out, people usually stroll by the river. It's a pastoral place, except for the stacks.

The church is full. The priest is making his way to the altar, and everyone is standing. But I am too tired to rise. I cannot hear, but I know everyone is singing. I know these people, they're the kind who take full part in the service.

But even though I cannot hear, I can see. I can see everything around me, and I can see in other places too. And sometimes I can see what is happening in other places better than where I am.

Just then someone gently touches my shoulder. I turn to look.

"Tired?" the woman asks.

From reading her lips, I can tell there's kindness in her voice. She's an older woman, someone I have known all my life. I must be related to her somehow – I am related to many people in this town. But I can't recall who she is.

Politely, I nod "yes" in reply.

"Well go on and rest then, my son. You need it."

They're good people, everyone. They would never want to hurt my feelings – they know I work nights – I have worked nights all my life. And they also know I never miss Mass; I am a good person. I am like them. They will let me remain seated; they'll allow me this little insurrection, even during the conse-cration, when everyone should be kneeling.

Today I am more tired than usual. But I have good reason to be – I have travelled many miles to get here. And it's when I am in this overtired state that I can see better than ever. I can see far and *beyond.*

The stacks are releasing something. *What?* Like steam. A slow re-lease, fumes that disperse easily. Then clean looking stacks again. But the river is something to watch, to keep an eye on. The swelling.

It's a slow rising. Still it's worrisome. The river.

I leave the pew, but I don't remember doing it. I don't re-member passing in front of the people sitting next to me. I don't recall going down the aisle, toward the nave and the tall wooden doors. I don't recall any of it.

But I am out by the river now. I am watching. I have to.

The waters are smooth, but already getting high. Will they rise to the top? I see the thin flow from the stacks, too. But the air is clean, white. The stacks are white, painted so clean.

But watch the water, the water. Watch the level. Watch how fast it's coming up now.

Suddenly I am back in the church. I am soft wings brushing against eyes, sweeping here and there, in the air... through the congregation, fluttering ... fluttering. Warning everyone.

But the people smile to themselves and brush me away. Hands, fingers. *What was that? What was that?* Vague thoughts that'll never transform into words. So wholesome is their con-centration in their ritual.

I am getting worried now. The water. The pure white stacks. The fullness of the church... I rush to the back, to the vestibule, where things are kept.

I find the bell... and even though it's a small one, it's still hard for me to lift. But I make myself do it. I have to. The bell must be made to ring and warn the people.

There. Clang, clang, clang...

But the sound is not loud enough. It's a sound that doesn't carry; a sound that doesn't go forth. It will not bring distraction to Holy Words.

Suddenly my deaf ears open to the people's singing, and as their voices rise in beautiful harmony, I find myself drawn to the music. It's my favourite hymn, and my heart fills with an intense spiritual yearning.

I wish I could join in the chorus... but I know I cannot remain here. I must tear myself away. I must not abandon my duties.

I hurry outside, to take one more look, to check on the state of things. But when I get there, I can't believe what I see. I can't believe how fast this thing is happening. The water has reached the top. It's rushing forward in a mindless swell.

There's nothing I can do anymore. There's nothing anyone can do. It's too late. The waters will not retreat.

Quickly, I gather my strength and give myself momentum, rising high in the air, higher than I have ever gone before. But I have to be careful not to get too tired and wear myself out. I have many miles to go before reaching home again.

Behind me, I can see the rolling of the water over the land... and the gloom of a dark *campanile*, where a large bell has been silent for years. But as soon as I gain some distance, I stop looking back... and the memory of a place I once knew so well, slowly fades into a comforting world of twilight.

No Man of Music

St. Anthony. Oh, St. Anthony. *'Na grazia...* a miracle I got you back. You made me strong, strong to cut the lock. Old, musty trunk no place for holy statue. You're with me again. You're my saint, my only saint.

You and me sit down now, here on soft chair. Old woman need much rest. Later, I go clean the mess, and hide what I done to get you back. Maybe I'll spread a fancy tablecloth on the trunk, the trunk with no more lock - large tablecloth that hang all the way to the floor - make it look like I want to pretty up the house. If Tony find out I take you out of there, Tony be angry; he not always a good son.

Yesterday, I look for key of trunk, look from morning till night. I know Tony don't carry it with him; I know he hide it somewhere inside. He clever boy - he almost twenty-five. But the key nowhere I can find. I was disappoint, but I went to bed anyway, because I felt so tire. My leg hurt bad, where he kick so many times.

"It's only an ugly relic," Tony say to me the other day. But I tell him he himself be named after St. Anthony and he should not speak bad about namesake saint - St. Anthony always there to look after him.

But Tony say he don't need no looking after by some freak who die a thousand years ago. I tell him St. Anthony take care of me real good, and I believe he sure exist. Tony get mad and yell, "I'm the one who takes care of you, you senile old woman... and I don't want no goddamn saint taking the credit. Do you hear?" And he grab St. Anthony away from me, and he throw him in the garbage, like my saint be some bad, evil thing.

I start to cry. I cry like the day I leave Italy and I know I never going to see my mama again.

"Okay, okay... shut up your wailing if you don't want me to smash the damn thing to the wall instead." And he go pick up St. Anthony from the garbage and he hold him rough in his hand.

"Yeah, yeah. Maybe that's what I'll do. Smash!" And he get ready to throw. "Make holy bits and pieces for you, Mama... I know you'll like that." And he laugh and laugh. But I can't see funny joke. I think he crazy, only he not *really* crazy... his eyes be really sad.

After he finish laugh like that, Tony change his mind: he no throw St. Anthony to the wall anymore, and he even start to talk a little bit kind. "Tell you what. I'll just lock the damn thing in the trunk. That is all I'll do. Just lock it up." He then explain that he have to do that, because old lady carrying a statue around all day and talking aloud to it, make him feel shame when his friends come.

Tony have many friends. He give parties all the time. He buy lots of beer and lots of wine. He feel real proud when he hear his friends say: "Eh, Tony! You macho man. How she going?"

Tony lucky fellow, for he no born ugly like his father...

When I was young, my papa say to me one day: "You marry Orfeo - he right man for you. Looks like he soon go to America - that very good thing." I answer him: "I will never marry Orfeo, because I no like nothing about him. He too old for me... and, anyway, I think he be the ugliest man in the village." But my papa very strict, and he say: "You do as I tell you or *else*." I have strong mind too, and I swear I go run away before the wedding. But Papa tell me there be no place to run. I think and think about that a lot and I afraid Papa very much right; I only fifteen, and I no educate… and I sure no have rich uncle in the city who would say to me: "You can come and live with us, Rosetta."

My mama say she can't do nothing to help, except carry big sorrow in her heart. She buy me wedding present; a little statue of St. Anthony of Padua – the saint people pray to when they *lost* something – he help you find. And she tell me: "Rosetta, you better not wear yourself out crying… sometimes things turn out not so bad. Maybe when Orfeo go to America something terrible happen to him – God forgive me for saying that – but maybe soon you'll be a rich widow." She too know how ugly Orfeo be, everyone can see.

A teacher lady I clean house for – after Orfeo go to America and he no send any support money – she say to me: "*Orfeo… Orfeo…* what a beautiful name." Her pretty face look like she dreaming wonderful dreams, and "*Orfeo*" she repeat again. Then she tell me about a man of long ago who was name Orfeo, too. She say he make the most beautiful music.

"He sure must have been a good player if people still remember him," I say.

She laugh soft, and she smile in her eyes. "*Si…* he *was* good – he used to sing, too… sing so good that men and creatures fell numb listening to him." She say they speak about him in books… she say there's a legend about him…

"No, my husband not like him," I tell teacher lady. "He no man of music… he no man of music at all."

But I tell her nothing else about my husband. Fine teacher lady sure no want to listen to peasant girl troubles. Maybe if I waste too much time talking, she give my job to somebody else – I need job bad, because I already tell people of the village that Rosetta no going to starve. No need they feel sorry for me, I told them, I can take care of myself. Even if I still very young, I no go begging for food. It no secret that Orfeo have another woman in America, and people glad about that. People of village be very mean sometime – maybe because they so poor. People who be poor for long time, sometime get strange mean in their heart.

The year Orfeo die, Tony ask: "Aren't you going to have Papa's picture put on his tombstone – everybody else does, all the other Italians in town?" I no wish to hurt him and tell him *no*, so I just say: "Your papa never take a good picture. He always too serious."

"You wouldn't want him smiling on his grave," Tony answer.

Tony sound much bitter. He no tell me why, and I no ask him either. But after that, he no talk about picture for tombstone anymore, and I glad. I want I should forget Orfeo – it not easy thing to do.

Right after the funeral, Tony ask so many questions, like he interest in everything sudden now. He want to know all about his papa and me.

I begin with the mistress. Orfeo have her five years... then one day he very mean to her, and she pack suitcase and she go away. She lucky woman – she have suitcase, and she have place to go!

"Then what happened?"

"Your papa wait six months, but when she no come back, he sent papers to Italy for me to come. He say I still his wife – vow in front of God not ever can be broken, he remind me."

"But how did you *know* about her – the other woman, I mean?"

I shrug. "No ocean ever stop gossip from travelling."

"So you just came?"

"Yes, that's what I do." But it not really exactly like that – I just no want to tell Tony big, long story.

Story be terrible memory. When papers arrive registered mail, I cry again like I cry the day I walk up to altar to marry Orfeo. I cry until my eyes be like the earth of summer forgot to rain. I don't know what to do anymore; now I be lost woman for sure - Orfeo in America and me in Italy not bad life - it be okay life to live till I die. But together with him be very bad. I sit looking at St. Anthony all day, but he no tell me nothing. I think he no want to give me miracle because I no pray same as other women do. I talk to him - that *my way* of pray. Only this time I so upset I no talk to him either. I be just like girl born dumb. But St. Anthony no forget me. One night when I can't sleep, he make good idea come to me.

Next morning, I hurry to next village. There live new priest; he the kind of priest who listen to women troubles very much - I hear say so by the women of our village. He no same as our old priest, they say. New priest be the kind that have a heart big and soft all the time.

When I arrive there, I find him outside the church. "What can I do for you, young woman?" he ask.

I quick down on my knees to tell whole sad story of arranged marriage. I beg him write letter to Orfeo in America for me. I say: "God forgive me *Padre*, but please you put down on paper careful right words... tell him it be best we not reunite." I tell young priest it okay by me if he tell Orfeo small lie... it okay tell him his pretty bride not pretty anymore. Tell him she grow very fat... maybe tell him she go a little crazy, too. Tell him she no right in her head at all - tell him she crazy bad.

Young priest say: "You don't need to be on your knees to ask me to do something for you." And with his own hand he help me to stand.

He make me go in his house by the church and he give me chair to sit. I very anxious for answer, while he think everything deep. He be a long time doing that, but when he finally speak again, he say: "The distress is plain on your face... leave me the man's address."

I want to kiss his feet.

After that, I very happy every day. I work for teacher lady in daytime, and I work in the fields in the evening. I work cutting wheat... and I always singing. At night I see beautiful stars - they so much the shiny kind.

Then one Sunday afternoon, loud knock come on my door. I go open wild fast. I think young priest be there to tell me I *free* - my heart jump so much.

Luck be against me. It be fat *Monsignore* stand there big. In his hand he have air mail letter. He holding it tight angry.

I feel like faint. I quick to guess what Orfeo done: he sent letter he receive from young priest to the church superior!

"You are a sinful woman!" *Monsignore* say like thunder. He stare.

I no be sinful... but I no say that to him. No woman ever talk back to fat *Monsignore* with large cross on his chest, and big ring on his finger.

What I to do now? I think and think.

But I no throw myself humble and sorry at his feet. It not true at all that I be a sinful woman. St. Anthony know - he keep everything listed in his book. He know I live like a virgin - I wish St. Anthony could speak!

But St. Anthony not be far away. He make a hen squawk in the chicken coop. *Monsignore* hear the hen, too, and I see in his eyes how much he like fresh eggs from the farm - he live in the city. He like everything from farm, that's how his reputation be. So I say to him: "Your *Eccellenza*, please come inside poor woman's house and rest - I go gather fresh eggs for you - the best in the village." I sure he be so glad to have fresh eggs that he forgive young priest for writing letter to Orfeo for me - I no want young priest in trouble. If I be in trouble, not so bad - my mama say women born to have trouble.

I give *Monsignore* a basket full of eggs, two dozen, maybe more - I too confuse to count. "These will make the best omelette," I tell him. "Maybe your servant woman will make you a big, tall cake, too - fresh eggs best for that for sure. Fresh eggs best for cook and for bake all the time... and if you come back next week, I give you more eggs - I save all of them for you."

Monsignore much changed now. He look like he taste delicious omelette already... sweet cake, too. He put his hand on my shoulder and he say maybe I not big sinner after all, maybe he make mistake about me. And if I go to confession soon, to old priest of my village, make sure, I be in grace of God again. And then after I finish doing big penance, I be ready to write letter to husband myself... and tell him I be very glad to start good marriage again, in America.

I think *Monsignore* ready to leave now, but I wrong. He turn around and he keep looking in my kitchen, like he want to make sure he no forget nothing. I can tell he want more fresh things, so I give him two bottles of olive oil, and one loaf of bread still warm from the oven. I help him carry everything to his car... and his chauffeur he take the gifts and put them careful on the back seat, and then makes ready to leave.

Soon, *Monsignore* riding away, and I waving to the back of his car. *He forget to give me his special Monsignore blessing. Maybe I no want it anyway.*

All night I no sleep. I no trust *Monsignore*, even after he take so much fresh stuff from me - I worry so much about young priest.

Before sun show face in the sky, I hurry to next village. But priest nowhere I can find... and priest house locked up. That strange... and I very upset. I sit on church steps.

I sit for a long time and I too afraid to think.

An old man with a donkey go by, and I quick ask, "Old man, tell me where I can find your priest..."

"Eh," he say, "you don't hear nothing? Everyone talking about him. He run away, and nobody know where he go. Some people say he went back to where he born, and some people say he went to Rome... but maybe he's on a ship to a far away place, that's what I say."

"Why he go? Hurry, speak!"

"Ah, too many are the stories people telling. But everyone say he take off his priest collar, after *Monsignore* tried to whip him. They say he do things a priest should never do... they say about a *letter* he wrote to a man in America..."

I already walking away. I no want to hear no more. It be never so sad a day before... it be the day Jesus got nails on his hands and his feet.

I go home. Young priest in trouble because of me. *St. Anthony protect him wherever he be. He good man. No matter he no have priest collar anymore... he still good man. He man with a soul.*

Nothing else to do now, but go to Orfeo in America - there just be no way out of terrible marriage. If I no go to America, Orfeo for sure come back to kill me - he man who talk of kill often when we first marry.

America not so bad - I surprised to be a little bit lucky again. When I arrive, Orfeo be sick with bad lungs and he no have much strength to beat me up - every time he try, he start coughing and can't stop. Cursing, he always fall back on his bed. He throw things at me, but that be all right - I always quick to move and he miss. Then soon he tell me I have to go to work. We need money bad, he say. They will take away the house if I don't start earning fast - Orfeo have a friend who find me work cleaning houses, like I do in Italy. It easy for me because I be with lots of experience.

When Orfeo's lungs get better, he go back to work - but he no work days anymore - he always go nights. That I like. This way I no have to sleep with him much - I always working daytime. But few times we in bed together, I be *real* careful: I no want to born sons or daughters from him. I be a pretty woman, and I so afraid I end up with ugly children.

When I forty-five, I sure know I born under bad star. It *happen*. I convinced it be a tumor and I soon be going to die, but instead the doctor say: "Everything is fine, Mrs. Pitro." And he smile. "You're pregnant."

Tony born big and strong, and I try to be good mother… but I so tire all the time. I say to Orfeo: "I need quit work to look after this child, because when I come home at night, too much things to be done - I no young anymore." But he reply: "Don't get no ideas, *shta gnoranda*. You born to work like a cow, so work and shut up."

Tony grow up. He smart boy, but sometimes he not happy… he very sad in his eyes.

Orfeo good to Tony. He say to him all the time, "Son, everything I have is yours." But he no have nothing. Money in bank no even enough to bury him… and the house not paid - Orfeo drink all his money away.

He drink mine, too. But I no angry for that - I glad Orfeo sitting in bars all weekends. It better for me when he no come home much - he ugly all his life.

Tony now get drunk, too, all the time. But he no go to bars; he only drink in the house. He sit in the living room and he drink until whisky bottle all gone. But when he have a party, he never drink - that strange about him. Maybe he like drink only when he alone. I no understand why.

And when Tony get really drunk, he always cry like a child. Once he cry for long, long time, and he say to me: "You never cared for my father... you never loved him." But I know Tony mean it different. I know Tony talking about himself. He really want to tell me that I never cared for *him*... that I never loved him.

But he don't know how much he wrong... and there be no way to make him see different – his mind too much made up now. It was Orfeo who turn Tony against me when he home all the time, after he retire. I don't know why he do it... maybe he want his son all to himself. Maybe he need somebody to love him special – he different than me – I lucky to have St. Anthony all the time for help me. I be very appreciate for the strength he give me – I always feel protected.

Orfeo use to take Tony fishing with him all the time... and he show him all the fishermen tricks. Father and son soon be real pals, talking to each other all the time, telling jokes and laughing. Once, when they be in the kitchen cooking fresh smelts, I want to taste some so bad, my mouth start watering. But Orfeo stop my hand from reaching the plate; he twist my wrist, twist until the bone almost break. Then he say to Tony: "We're not going to let her have fish that *we* caught, are we, son? She don't deserve any... she big bitch who don't love people... she no *need* people – she never did. She's got her saint."

Tony look like he want to tell his papa to stop hurting me, but he not sure he should do it. I know he want to stay big pal with his papa – that important to him. So he just look the other way and go back to turning the fish in the fry pan, to make them cook real well.

• • •

There. Tony coming home now - he all finish work. He un-locking back door.

"You still around, old lady?" he shout, when he hear big silence in the house. "You're not dead yet?"

Tony get nervous when I tell him that women in my family all got strong heart and never one of them die young. They all be ninety or a hundred.

"Maybe she really croaked this time," he say to himself. Then much louder, "No, she wouldn't give me the satisfaction. Come on, where are you hiding?"

I stay quiet - I no move.

Tony go back outside. He make four trips to his car. I know he carry beer and he carry wine. Tonight be Friday night... it be big party night.

"Well, now. Where is my goddamn supper, old lady?" he yell from the kitchen. "Don't tell me you fuckin' forgot again!"

He very mean when he angry. He angry now. Maybe he going to kick my leg and bust a vein, like he do the other time.

Tony go in his bedroom now. He bang door really loud. That's when I sudden remember: *the trunk... it still be open since I take little statue of St. Anthony out... the saw still there on the floor of the hallway, too.* Tony know for sure now what I done - it plain to see. I fast to hide St. Anthony under my shawl.

Tony coming to living room now. He stand stiff in the doorway. Better that my heart stop now; *dead* I be all right. Dead I would feel nothing. Sometime I be a weak woman: sometime I afraid of the way he going to hurt me.

I no like the way Tony be smiling. He have smile too big for his teeth. It much too sweet smile, too. It not be Tony natural smile.

"So, you really want your little saint, ah? Well, you can keep the little fellow. It don't hurt me none. None at all. I got other things on my mind tonight."

I say nothing. I no understand the way he act now. It be new way. He never be like this before. He angry before, he mean… but he never be soft polite.

"Yep… big things on my mind. This is party night, remember? Well, it's going to be party all over the house. Maybe the house won't even be big enough. That's right, that's how big it's going to be. Yes sir, *Mama*."

"If party too big, police come."

"Never - not when Tony gives a party. I know how to keep things under control. Tony is *boss* here. Everyone listens when Tony gives orders. Yes sir."

"Maybe Tony too much big boss."

"Me? No, Mama. Tony knows just how far to go."

He have smile in front of his teeth, again. "And I am considerate, too… that's why I thought that tonight you should sleep in the basement… so I can be private with my friends, and you can be private with your jolly dolly saint. Fair deal, *Mama*?"

"My bladder… there no bathroom in basement."

"Oh, don't worry… plenty of buckets down there. You can keep one handy by the old sofa… You're not going to cry now, are you? No, my mama wouldn't cry over anything but her little saint, would she? No she wouldn't break down now… not when she didn't even cry a tear when her husband died. *Did she*?"

"You put furnace up - basement cold."

"Eh Christ, have pity. We'll be sweatin' up here. You know how it is with the booze and the fast music. Yes sir, it'll be a hot night tonight."

"I go cook supper for you now."

"Uh-uh. No need anymore. I'll order pizza for myself. No muss and no fuss. You go right along now. Time for your rest."

"I get blanket from bedroom."

He pull me back, rough. "Shame, shame. You got no faith in your little saint to keep you warm? But don't worry, I'll throw you down a blanket - *later on,* if you're a good girl that is. Come now, no time to waste. Here, let me help you to the stairs. *Da,* give Tony you hand... you go nighty nighty."

He open door of basement... and he bare his teeth like he crazy man locked up. I know now he not *normal* of mind.

He give me big shove, and slam the door shut.

I no fall - I very quick to grab hand railing. Statue still under my shawl. I very strong.

Faces in the Window

The accordion was the only thing he had left that mattered. His house was good, made of bricks and plaster. All the houses around him were gone. The last one to go had been poor August's place. That's where they built the L-shaped old folks' home, on his four acres.

There had been things to do then, taking walks and arguing about this and that, sitting on the verandah, until the silence fell.

He'd said to him one day: "August, when we get older and more than half crippled, we should live together at my house or yours - take care of each other."

He didn't say anything for a long time and Sam figured he was thinking it over. August was that way, nothing impulsive about his manner - a good, wise Polishman.

But the next time they were together, August picked a peach from Sam's orchard and polished it to a velvet before he said: "It can't be, Sam. I didn't want to tell you, but I've got this cancer in my stomach… it hurts pretty bad some days, and when I go to the hospital I won't come back. It will be just you, Sam."

After that it was so hard to chit-chat, the cancer always there, in his friend's stomach, growing, getting bigger, and Sam never being able to forget it.

Then it happened. Like a dream he was gone.

His son came from out West to sell the house. He sold it cheaply so he could get home soon. He wasn't even back on the plane when a crew came to tear the house down, what was left of his friend's existence.

Looking at the place where the house had stood, at times made Sam wonder if he had really known a man named August. It was such a different view, the land.

Time passed and one day he couldn't remember August's face at all; it was lost forever like so many others before him.

Now he went to look around in the stores all day long, the fancy mall nearby. There, he met the sons and daughters of his old acquaintances, most of them not remembering his name and anxious to get away. But they all recalled where he lived, for he had been in the same house for forty-five years, and they said he was lucky that they were building a senior citizens' home in the empty land next to him, because it could have been a smelly fish and chip place or a noisy drive-in.

When the building had a roof and all and it came to be inhabited, he knew they had been right. Everything was so clean and kept up and no smells at all… and the nurses that went in and out and the visitors were neat and tidy.

Only the old ones in there were disheveled.

He knew that since the time his music drew them to the windows to watch. There were three large windows facing his backyard. It was there that he began to play again after so many years, first in the daytime and then when he couldn't catch sleep at night. Sitting on a straight chair in the little clearing among his fruit trees, old songs came back to his fingers like something he'd never forgotten.

Then the first palsied face came, after the light sprang on and the blind rolled up, to stare at what it could see past the new fence, the old man stretching the accordion between the low branches. Soon, another face and the light in the other room and the other, two faces in each window, like frightened children been in the woods too long.

He serenaded them in the late night when the sun was giving light to another world and the moon was a faded blossom drooping above his orchard. And he saw their eyes twinkle, each pair of them, the eyes of all the ones who had gotten old before him and gone. He played and played until he saw his fingers become slim and his body young and full of rhapsody that flowed down his leg and his foot like a soft drum that touched the earth with it.

Then he saw them arrive, the nice policeman who'd come to make him go inside and take a rest, and another stalwart with him. But tonight he couldn't stop, he had to keep playing, for he remembered their faces, how they hung over sadly when the lawman had said, "Please Pops, you're disturbing the peace," and begged him to fold away the instrument.

He couldn't disappoint them, like he'd never disappointed anyone, not August and not all the others, and he made the accordion dance in his arms and the sound spread, dissolved all around, absorbed by the new brilliance of the stars, the softening of the night, the joy-beating tempo of their hearts...

Cinzia

I wondered what my mother would think of Cinzia... and what Cinzia would think of my mother. I could tell as soon as she arrived that things wouldn't be smooth. There would be trouble. My brother's new wife was not like the other brides from Italy.

There were four of them on our street. Sometimes they congregated on the front porch of the house across from us, where one of them lived. If I happened to be on our front porch, reading, they would call me to go over and sit with them. They said why would I want to sit alone when I could be in the company of grown women. But when I got there, they usually forgot all about me, and I would have to pretend to be examining the split ends at the bottom of my braids. They all had big bosoms, and they talked very loud. The things they said made me blush so much sometimes that I would get up and go lean over the railing and watch the bees sucking on the sweet buds of the purple and white holly hocks that grew between the driveway and the porch.

Only one of them used to be kind of quiet. I knew she loved her husband because she would never talk about him, about what they did in bed at night. She said they were happy, and that was all she needed to tell. But the others all jeered and said she was being stuck up. They laughed when they said that, but still I knew there was a lot of meanness and jealousy behind it.

I wondered if Cinzia loved my brother. But I guess she didn't, because not even four months later, she started having an affair with a Russian fellow who lived behind us. The man was not married and lived with his mother, who was very old. He started talking to Cinzia along the fence, where she spent a lot of time patiently breaking up the earth around the flowers she had planted. She wanted to make sure they didn't die, for she had planted them against my mother's advice... my mother who was convinced nothing could survive in that kind of soil. It was hard like rocks.

One day Cinzia was seen going across to the man's house. Two women on our street, who had been watching, immediately came to report everything to my mother. They had a very good reason to keep a close eye on things they said, since there was a lot to suspect already. How could a girl as beautiful as Cinzia, who also had the start of a good education to her credit, be happy in a simple household like ours? There was no doubt in their minds that she had used her marriage to my brother as a passport to Canada – Cinzia's father had suddenly died the year before, leaving his wife and three daughters to figure out how best to survive. Cinzia was sixteen at the time, and the oldest of the daughters. Yes, there was bound to be unfaithfulness on the part of this young woman... and what's more, the Russian was very handsome.

The next day my mother demanded to know from Cinzia why she had gone to the man's house. Cinzia looked the other way and said he was helping her with English – the man could speak several languages, even Italian.

"You're lying," my mother said. "*Puttana*. That's what you are. You don't deserve to be a mother to my son's children."

Cinzia didn't say anything; she just stared out the window. I wished she would say something to defend herself, but I guess she *couldn't*, and the next day she went back to the man's house again. After that, she went there almost every day. When I got home from school, around four o'clock, she was usually coming back across the yard – the Russian worked nights and was always home in the day-time. I tried to cover up for her whenever I could, but it wasn't easy. Happening to be at home during a religious holiday and caught lying about where Cinzia had been that afternoon, my mother was furious, tempted to slap me. "Protecting a whore," she accused. "Why do you do it? Why?"

I had no answer to give her. No answer that I could give myself either. I just liked Cinzia, and that was all. I could have never done anything to hurt her. Maybe it was the way she had put her arms around me and held me close to her one day, after fixing my hair, pinning it all up in pretty curls.

"Here," she whispered, letting me hold the silver-handled mirror she had brought with her from Italy. "Turn around and look at the back. You look like a little princess."

"But I'll never be as beautiful as you."

That's when she held me tight and cried on my shoulder, little sobs coming and going, the scent of perfume, like violets, from her neck, her breasts...

"*Piccolina*," she cried. "You're the only one I can *tell*. I miss my little sister. I miss my family..."

"But you'll go back to see them soon," I said. "Or they'll come to see you."

"Yes, I wish that," she whispered, her cheeks gleaming with the wetness of huge tears.

I didn't know Cinzia was going to have a baby, until her belly was big enough to tell. We had always been a quiet family, but now there were hardly any words spoken at all around our place anymore. Just the necessary things, and even then there were gestures and sign language.

"Jesus Christ, I don't understand you," my father said to my brother one morning. "How can you just sit back and do nothing?" My bedroom was next to the kitchen and I could hear everything. "If she were my wife, I'd kick her with my boots and send her flying down the street. And she wouldn't be coming back, either. Not even if she begged on her knees!"

My father had a right to be angry, but suddenly I knew I never wanted to sit close to him anymore. I'd never want to sit on his lap again, as I always did... and feel the roughness of his beard when he hadn't shaved for a few days. I couldn't bear the thought of his arms around my shoulders, as he pulled me close to him... the gentle kiss he always planted on my forehead just before he pushed me back down... What my father wanted to do to Cinzia was terrible. I never wanted him to touch me ever again.

Joe's lunch bucket was made of steel, and I heard him snatch it from the table. "You think I'm crazy?" he shouted. "You think I want to end up in jail and ruin my life for a woman? This is Canada, not Italy."

"And what about your honour... how can that change from one country to another? Tell me that!"

"Are you coming or not?" My brother was a carpenter like my father and they both worked on the same construction site. "If you don't hurry up, I'm going."

"Go then. I'll stay home. And I won't need you anymore. I'm going to buy my own car."

"Oh, now you're going to buy your own car. What's that going to do?"

"I'll tell you what it's going to do. I won't have to ride back and forth to work every day with a fool."

"Well, it's your goddamn fault I married her."

"Oh, now it's my fault. What next?"

"And Mom's…"

"Oh, your mother's fault, too."

"That's right. Think about it."

About a month later, Cinzia stopped going over to her lover's house. His mother was very ill, and he was spending all his spare time at the hospital. I wondered what was going to happen to Cinzia; I worried about her every day. I hoped the old lady would hurry up and die so that her son could take Cinzia away. I was afraid of what would happen to her if she stayed in our house. My parents never spoke to her anymore, and my brother pretended she didn't even exist. I was too afraid to be nice to her in front of them in case they would get *really* angry and beat me up.

"We were a decent family, and look at us now," Mama said one day. "Where can we hide our faces?" But actually my mother was stronger than my father; gossip didn't humble and subdue her at all. She would walk down the street with her head held high, eyes straight ahead. At home, she almost took pride in cursing the people she imagined to be rejoicing in our terrible disgrace.

"*Maledetti*," she cursed. "I hope God will strike them blind for their viper's tongues." And with that, she proceeded to give a mock spit over her shoulder in defiance.

But with my father it was different. He couldn't handle the way people stared at him and talked behind his back, the pity from his friends. It got so bad that he stopped going to Mass on Sunday, and he never went near the Sicilian club to play cards with his *paesani* anymore. Except for work, he stayed home all the time.

The tension in our house was unbearable… yet, strangely, Cinzia grew more beautiful every day. Her skin was soft and pink as that of the child I imagined she was going to have. Sometimes, completely lost in thought, she would stand in the middle of the kitchen, and loosely join her hands below her stomach, white fingertips opening and closing like petals...

"So, I see you have made up your mind to support another man's child," my mother said to Joe one night, while Cinzia had gone for a walk. I was sitting there doing my homework.

My brother picked up the kitchen scissors and began cutting his nails. "Not quite," he replied.

"Well then, what are you going to do?"

"I'm leaving... going away."

My mother stopped rolling out the pasta she was making for our next day's meal. She lifted her head and stared.

"And who is going to take care of Cinzia and the baby?" I cried, worried. Afraid.

"It's none of your business, little girl. In fact, you shouldn't even be listening. But since you asked, I'll tell you," he said, a strange smile on his lips. "Mom and Dad are the lucky people."

My mother blinked, as if a handful of dirt had hit her eyes. "What's that supposed to mean?" she cried.

"It means that I did my part. You wanted me to go back to Italy to get a wife... so I went back to Italy and got a wife. And now our beautiful Cinzia is all yours."

My mother stared at him with her mouth open. But then she put her head down and started rolling out the pasta again. I could tell from her expression that she had to do a lot of thinking before she could bring herself to speak again. But I couldn't wait, I just couldn't.

"You're terrible! Don't you care about her at all?" I cried, my eyes suddenly filling with tears. "How can you just go away and leave her like that?"

My brother lifted one of my braids, and brushed the tip of my nose with it - one of his teasing gestures, now almost turned mean by anger and resentment. "How can I, you say? Very easy. I don't love her, and she doesn't love me."

"What's love got to do with it? Cinzia needs someone to take care of her. She's going in the hospital to have the baby in a month, and nobody will even go see her. It's awful. You're all so mean! You're evil!"

"Well, if you feel like that," Joe said, throwing the scissors on the counter, "maybe you can look after her. How is that?"

"Well, I will," I shouted, running outside sobbing. "I will!"

• • •

It was dark and they had not found me. I would hide from them forever. I would make them hurt the way they were making me hurt. I would show them how horrible they were, the terrible things they were doing to poor Cinzia. Hours passed and night fell.

It was Cinzia who found me. "I *knew* you were in the tool shed all the time," she laughed. "But they wouldn't tell me anything. They wouldn't even ask me to help look for you. I had to figure out on my own what was going on, what was happening." She gave a deep sigh. "Like all the rest... like everything else since I came here. They don't like anything about me, anything I do. They don't want me to be smart... have brains of my own. Anyway, what's the use. But you... do you want to stay here, or do you want to come out?"

"I don't know."

"Well, you've got to make up your mind sometime."

"Well, I won't."

I was sitting on the floor, and I looked up. I could hear her breathing. I could smell her violet perfume... In the shadows, her belly was like a mountain above me. What if the baby would drop out of her now? What would I do? I didn't know anything... I didn't understand anything about women giving birth. The baby could die!

I wanted to ask her if it was true about the Russian; I wanted to *know*. After all, it could be a lie... a lie that had spread until it was too large to take back, a lie that was everyone's lie and nobody's lie, like chains and circles all tangled up... a falsehood no longer possible to deny. But somehow the words that finally came out of me had nothing to do with her lover: they had to do with us, our family.

"Why did you come to Canada," I blurted out angrily. "Why did you have to come and ruin everything in our lives?"

There was complete silence for a long time. Then after a little sigh, she took her sweater off and dropped it down over my knees. "Don't get chilled... it wouldn't be a good time to get sick." And I listened, as her slippered feet padded back toward the house.

I began to hit the floor with my fists, letting the rough cement rip my flesh over and over again, until I could feel the blood, like thick juice, around my fingers... my palms, wrists. The pain was dull. I touched my face, rubbed it.

I was told later that it was my brother who carried me inside... and what I remember, like a dream and only like a dream, is my mother tearing a clean white pillow case, to make bandages... and my father holding the bowl of water for Cinzia, who kept sponging me with her velvet hands.

The Vineyard

"Don't," I say. "Don't you ever say that to me again. Do you hear me?"

But I know in my mind the reproach is futile even before it is spoken.

He utters the words again. Softer this time. Cunningly. Knowing exactly what they'll do to me: *Fuck off.*

I want to scream and call him names, the anger so deep. But it's not in me to raise my voice too much. I was brought up by gentle folk, whose words were always kept low.

"You'll have to be the one to make it work," my mother said to me once, almost in a whisper, after I complained about my husband's sporadic drinking and his foul mouth. "He was raised different... he's not like us. His people are what they are... and he was born from those people, just like you were born from us."

I leave the kitchen, slamming the door behind me. I know it's not much retaliation where my husband is concerned, but I never used to slam doors before. I started doing it only this year, when our son went into his teens. I feel ashamed of my anger, an anger that could kill.

I lie in bed, stiff. Arms crossed around myself, pressing soft hardness. My own breasts... bigger than they really are. Full of mother love... of woman love. What to do. Always caught between father and son. Am I the one who's always wrong? How can that be?

I cross my feet, too. Bone upon bone. Lay me on a plank, one straight and one across. Lay me there on Jesus' cross.

Or lay me upon the twigs...

A big bed of twigs, cut from the vineyard. My father cutting and trimming... snip, snip, making ready for the new growth in the spring. Sharp, dark steeled snips. Mama carrying bundles on her head, moving slowly across the fields.

Eyes follow. A little girl. Skip and jump. Run errands. Watch. Follow soft steps... Mama moving through vapours, the sun drawing dampness high up into the hills.

"Watch your brother," Mama says. "Watch how he stacks the bundles. Someday it'll be your turn... We'll burn the pile tonight, when the work is done... Vine twigs are useless in the chimney – we're blessed with better kindling."

The burning was quick. Shoot and crackle, like firework on the ground. The day was long waiting... and the flames shot up quick and hungry, toward the sky. In no time the fire was gone... the ashes flimsy, easily blown away by the wind.

"Look," he blurts out, rough getting into bed, yet trying to smooth the sheets between us almost to a silly perfection. "It's just a goddamn word... why can't you understand? It's not when I drink that bothers you... nor whatever the hell we're arguing about... but just the goddamn words that mean nothing. I was brought up with them – and for years I kept my tongue tied for you. But now that son of ours is driving me crazy, and the words just come back to me. Words, it's the only weapon I got. I am sorry, I went too far tonight."

I turn the other way, and stare at the dark wall.

"Say something, for God's sake."

But I can't speak just yet. How can I, when I am still staring through time, at the spot where the pile burned? The ashes are all gone... but the ground is still charred. It will take a few seasons before the grass will grow again... where the flames sparked.

"Maybe tomorrow," he says. "Okay?"

And I am glad for the sound of his voice.

Before You Leave

I was ready for bed when the doorbell rang. I knew who it was, who it had to be. No one else would come to see me that late.

"Hello, Sam," Michael said. "I wasn't sure if you'd still be up. Can I come in?"

I could have said no, but I didn't. Instead, I led the way to the family room and watched him sit down.

"So, she had it," he said without wasting any time. "The baby."

I suppose he had heard about it at the Caboto Club. It was a good place for news, for anything that happened around town.

"You shouldn't be driving," I told him. I knew he had been drinking; I could tell from the colour on his cheeks. Wine always put a flush to them. "You'll lose your license…"

"Don't worry about me, Sam. Actually, I didn't drive. I walked. I've been walking for a long time. I needed to do a lot of thinking. I needed to work things out in my mind."

I didn't say anything for a long time. He didn't either. Then I decided to break the silence. "So you did thinking… to solve what?"

"Not solve… maybe just learn to live with it."

"Sure," I said. I wasn't trying to be sarcastic. I just didn't know what else to say.

"They told me it was a boy," Michael said. "Were you surprised... I mean everyone else seems to be having girls, lately."

"No, not really. We already knew it would be a boy. Nowadays there's nothing one doesn't know ahead of time... except when someone else is fooling around with your wife."

"Go ahead... stick needles in my heart. I deserve it... Do you have anything to drink in the house? We might as well celebrate. It isn't the child's fault."

I didn't want to, but I did it. I went down to the cellar and brought up a bottle of home-made wine. I took a glass out of the cupboard and put it beside the bottle on the coffee table. "Help yourself," I said, gesturing with my hand.

He looked at me for a second, then got up and went to get another glass. "We should stick together," he said, filling both glasses.

"Why should we?"

"Because we're family."

I picked up my glass. "Families have respect for each other," I replied, slowly sitting down on the rocking chair by the fireplace. I rocked back and forth for a while.

"Nice chair," he said, coming to refill my glass. I had emptied it pretty fast.

"I bought it last week... for her to rock the baby in."

"Yeah, I thought it was new."

I looked at my hands and they were shaking. Then I told him she had called his name when she was in labour. I couldn't have lived with myself if I hadn't told him.

"So what?" he shrugged, looking away. "Women do things like that all the time. They say one thing for another. They get mixed up."

After that we both kept silent for a long time. We both knew the truth now and it was worse than not knowing. We had to do something.

"Take her away," I said to him at last. "Just take her and the baby and go."

He stared across the room. The glass trembled in his hand and wine spilled on his pants. "You still don't understand. I don't love Maria. I told you that before. It was a mistake... a moment. We were both lonely. You were away for so long on that last job... and I had just broken up with Selina. That's the way it was. That's all."

"Oh sure, that's all. That's the way it was, eh? You put a child into the world and you don't even love the woman... What's the matter, isn't Maria good enough for you? Tell me that!"

"Sam, I didn't come here to fight. You already know that."

"So why did you come... to bring me greetings?" My glass was empty again and I refilled it myself this time.

"Don't get drunk, Sam. You know how you always get feeling sad when you drink..."

He had no sooner finished saying that when my eyes began to fill with tears. Michael was right about me when I got drunk... and for a moment I thought I was going to sob.

"Take it easy," Michael said. "Maybe I do love Maria. But not the way you do. I am just not the type to settle down. I am not like you... steady... solid as a rock."

"Go away," I said, mopping my eyes with my handkerchief. "Go away and never come back."

"Yeah, Sam," he said, getting up. "That's why I came by. I came to tell you I am going away... and I wanted to see if you wanted me to leave you my new address."

"What for? Why would I want that?"

"I don't know. Like I said before, we're family."

"No," I said firmly. "I have no need for it... But Maria might want it. I think you should see her before you leave."

He put his head down. For a minute he looked like he was

going to cry, but he didn't. Michael had always been strong that way. He could hold it all in.

"Okay," he said, at last. "I'll do it. But only because you're older than I am... because you think I should."

Then we shook hands and said good-bye. I wished him good luck... and told him to be careful crossing the street. He said he would, and left.

He wasn't walking too badly. Actually, he carried his wine better than I did. That was one thing I had to admit about my brother, he could always walk straight no matter what. He knew how to keep going...

From the window, I watched him disappear around the corner. Then I pulled down the blinds and slowly went to sit in the rocking chair.

Visions

"We have to go," says Frank. "We have to go and do this thing… we have to go and pick it out. She has left it up to us, and there isn't much time."

"Yes, I know," says Eric. "But I've been thinking. I would like to do something different."

"What do you mean?"

"I'd like to paint it. I'd like to do a painting on it. Like a mural."

"Are you serious?"

"Of course, I am serious."

"Oh God. That's you… not an once of your brain with a practical thought attached to it."

"I still would like to do it," Eric says. "I think it would look great."

"I can just imagine!"

"Well, he was my father, too… and I have a right. And I bet *she* wouldn't mind - Mom. She would like it."

"That's because she's as crazy as you are. Eccentric. Nuts!"

But as soon as he says that, he gives his brother a quick glance. Frank is not sure if he can trust Eric just now. His younger brother has a temper that can flare up at the most unpredictable time.

Eric looks at him. "You say that again and I'll punch you."

But it's a mild threat, Eric's tone almost benevolent.

He's not stupid, Frank thinks. He knows he can't do what he wants to do without my approval, so he'll play the game. He will not allow himself to explode, if he can help it.

Suddenly Frank gets up from the sofa and goes into the kitchen. He opens the liquor cabinet and takes out a bottle.

Paint it, he thinks. The idiot wants to paint it. God, what next?

It would be some funeral all right... a dead man laid to rest in a painted coffin! Maybe they should have a parade, too... tour the streets of town, reporters and TV cameras on the spot. Frank makes his drink a double shot.

Eric comes to stand at the kitchen door. "Well, what do you think?"

"I think you're crazy, that's what I think!"

"I am not crazy... and you know it."

Still desperately hoping to dissuade him, Frank decides to try a different approach. "Look, Eric... it's not so much that I am against it... but it's not even possible. Caskets have a lacquered surface... paint probably won't even stick them." .

"Oh, don't worry about that. I'll roughen it up, sandpaper it. I'll even have it sandblasted if I have to."

"You won't give up, will you? Anyway, they probably won't let you do it - the funeral home people."

"I'll find out. Frank... I *have* to do it - I need to."

"Why? What for?"

"I don't know. I just have to. Maybe because I care. Don't you care?"

"Well, now! What the hell do you think I have been doing all these years, while you were slapping paint on canvasses? Who do you think went to pick him up from the bars all the time, when he was stinking drunk?"

"I'm sorry. I didn't mean to imply anything."

Frank takes a big gulp from his drink. "And do you think it was easy… is that what you think?"

"No, I don't think that. But what makes you think it was any different for me? At least, you, being older, had a few good years with him before he got really bad."

"Sure. Big deal."

"Well, okay. But the least we could do at a time like this, if we were going to have a drink, is to have a drink together."

"Oh, I'm sorry," Frank says. And he goes to the cupboard and takes out a glass for his brother, hands him the bottle of brandy. "I wasn't thinking."

"It's all right. But we'd better be careful. Not to drink too much that is. We don't want to turn out like him."

"Don't worry. Especially now that I am a father myself… I would never want to do that to my child."

"I know you wouldn't, Frank… but maybe Dad didn't want to either. I don't think he meant to hurt his family."

Frank looks at Eric for a minute, and then slowly dumps the remainder of his drink in the sink. "Well, especially nowadays, with the world as messed up as it is, a child doesn't need any extra burdens."

"Yeah… and death is so final," Eric says, absently.

"For an artist, that's sure some original thought."

"Yeah, well. That's as original as I can get at a time like this. But you… now that you have a child…"

"Now that I have a child, what?"

"Well, you see… I don't think I could bear to have a child."

"What do you mean by that? Why couldn't you bear to have a child?"

Eric stares at his own hands, the way they're shaking. "Because I think about death a lot, you know."

"No, I don't know."

"Damn it, you do know. You're not without fears. You just don't want to show that you're afraid, that's all. You think you need to be strong all the time. But sometimes... " Eric breaks off. He can't finish speaking, and his eyes are already full with tears.

Frank goes back to the living room, sits down and lowers his head. His hands come together in a tight grip.

"Oh shit," says Eric, as he quickly wipes his eyes and goes to sit beside his brother.

"Frank, I didn't mean to get you upset. I know how much little Noah means to you... I hope I didn't make you think of anything ever happening to him..."

He doesn't say anything for a long time. But when he finally speaks again, his voice is a gentle murmur. "You're right about me. I never wanted to know what it's like to feel pain..., but with Dad gone just like that... well... Anyway, I don't want to talk about it. I am not like you. I can't just bring it all to the surface. Just can't."

"But that's okay. You don't have to be like me. It's good that we're different."

"Anyway, if anything should happen to my little son, I don't know what I would do."

Eric lets his hand rest on his brother's arm. "Everything will be all right. Nothing is going to happen to Noah. Nothing is going to happen to anyone."

"I hope you're right."

"I am. You'll see."

"Yes," Frank says, "and now, I suppose we should get back to the subject."

"Yes, I think we should. It's not something that can be put off - a funeral."

Frank smiles a little. "It's not the funeral - it's what you want to do."

"It's not as weird as you think. In ancient times they used painted coffins."

"Yeah, well, ancient times… and where?"

He tries to imagine a painted coffin, but he can't. He sees it stripped of it's glossy finish… sees the grain of the wood… but that's as far as his mind will take him. For a moment he envies his brother's perception… the force of his imagination, his visions.

"So what would you paint on it," he asks.

"I don't know. I'd just let my hands create."

He shakes his head, then laughs. "How am I supposed to understand?"

"Maybe you're not supposed to."

"Maybe not. You're right. But I suppose I could agree to it."

"You know what? I think you could, too," says Eric, offering his hand.

Frank looks at his brother's trembling hand, and takes it and holds it, squeezes it tight. Then they both put their jackets on and head out the door. They're late for their appointment at the funeral home, but only a few minutes. Everything will be all right.

Don't Forget Tomorrow

The dining room is full. The wheelchairs are squeezed around the table, and the terry cloth bibs are in place. Waiting makes them quiet.

"Oh, it's so good to see so many of you here today," smiles Jean, pleased.

As the activity co-ordinator of the chronic care ward, she puts a lot of effort into enticing the patients to come out of their rooms as much as possible.

Cards big as menus are passed around to say grace. Only three or four persons utter the words; the rest just stare at the prayer printed in large block letters.

The food cart is parked out in the hall. The aroma emanating from it is overpowering.

"Beef soup... good!" gurgles a young man whose speech is quite impaired.

Two volunteers arrive to help, and trays are brought around the tables. Almost everyone is anxious to start eating. They go at it as best as they can. Shaky fingers lift the lids from the plates. The ones with only one good hand open the salt and pepper packets with their forks. The nurses assist only when it's necessary, allowing the patients to do as much as they can for themselves. An Alzheimer's patient eats his dessert first; then, after it's all gone, he licks his sticky fingers and moans in a soft manner.

Before dinner is over a middle-aged man comes to the door of the dining room. He's tall and good-looking, and is wearing a navy blue raincoat over his suit. His hair is well trimmed and he is holding his hat in his hands. Jean has never seen him before, but then she has been working there only a few months.

"Gisele," calls one of the nurses. "Gisele dear, your husband is here."

The woman lifts her head. She stares at the tall windows and laughs in a vacant tone of voice. Then: "Oh, is he? Is he here?" Her spoon fiddles with a small piece of Jell-O on her plate.

Gisele is in her fifties, but is aging in an uneven and peculiar way. Her voice has remained clear and bright as that of a young woman, while her body is already quite old – her face and her hands seem to have been buffed smooth of wrinkles.

"Gisele has come to join us," Jean says to the man. "We're so pleased. She usually doesn't want to leave her room. She's so attached to it. Aren't you, Gisele?"

Gisele laughs and laughs.

There are plenty of chairs around for visitors, but the man doesn't sit. He glances about the room. There are large paper ghosts hanging from the ceiling, and the walls are done up with witches and skeletons.

"Gisele is really good at cutting things out with the scissors. Aren't you, Gisele?" says Jean.

She giggles. Then, speaking to nobody in particular, says, "Yeah, trick or treat."

In a wheelchair, a young woman squirms. She lets out a shrill scream; but no one pays attention to her.

110

The empty trays are being taken away one by one. A cozy contentment prevails among the patients.

Jean turns her attention to the visitor, but he has disappeared. And when she goes out in the hallway, to talk to someone at the nurses' station, she sees him standing by the elevator, waiting for it to stop. He is impatiently beating his leg with his hat.

Back in the dining room, the nurses are starting to take the patients back to their rooms for their afternoon naps. Gisele is still bright eyed, so she'll be the last one to go. Jean sits by her and strokes the smoothness of her hand. "Don't forget tomorrow. Halloween, remember?" Gisele gives a happy laugh. "Popcorn... candy..."

"I'll check with the nurses about the popcorn," replies Jean. "Popcorn could be hard to swallow. But lots of goodies for sure."

Soon the dining room is empty and Jean stands there alone for a minute. Some days it's so hard to force herself not to think about the patients in there. But that's what she must do if she wants to be able to carry on. Sighing, she stares at the hollowed-out pumpkins resting on the window sill. *She was supposed to remember something – something that she must do. What was it?*

"Oh yes," she says aloud, as it comes back to her. She must see if she can find some candles for the jack-o'-lanterns, before the day is over.

Talk About Roses

Ialways wanted to write fiction. But how can I write fiction when there's so much real stuff happening?

Last night she called me and said, "Vincey, I need somebody. I can't handle it all alone. Would you come over?"

Of course I told her I'd be there. What could I do? Would you have refused? Would anyone, under the circumstances...

When I got there, she was shivering. She was standing with a blanket wrapped around herself... and I took her in my arms like a flower... I know, maybe I am trying to be poetic. A flower. What kind of flower would be that big? A sunflower maybe. Not quite. A sunflower would be tall but not wide... at least not as wide as Susan now. A real little whale she is. And she still has three months to go.

"Why," she cried. "Why did it have to happen?"

I say: "Hush, darling." But she isn't my darling. Not anymore. At least she wasn't before this thing happened. Before the accident. She had chosen Jerry over me.

Yes, she had done that all right.

I don't want to remember. I don't even want to tell you, or

anyone else for that matter, how she had slowly worked the ring out of her finger and given it back to me. It was not easy for her. Oh, I know how difficult it must have been. For five years we'd been together. Not living together. But together - inseparable.

"It's such a beautiful diamond," she said, "and I don't want to mail it in case something should happen to it. Please take it."

Finally I held out my hand, the way I do when I go to communion down at Sacred Heart Church, where we were to be married next June.

And then she folded my fingers over the ring and said, "You'll make some girl really happy someday, Vincey."

She was gone and I was still holding my hand closed, as if by opening it I would let the last thread of hope fly into the sky forever. And so with my hand fisted like that I walked home.

I didn't go straight home though. Home was only four blocks away from the park where we had been walking; home was too close. So I walked to other places. Other streets. Other parts of town. I walked for hours.

I am not sure where I lost the ring; I never went back to look for it.

"I'm pregnant," she said to me one day. "Listen to me Vincey... you have to listen. I am going to have a baby."

"Oh, that's a good one," I replied. "We don't make love for three months and suddenly you're pregnant."

"Vincey, stop that. Stop it!"

I knew then. I knew it for sure that someday I might be the godfather of this baby, but certainly not the father. For sure not that.

And you know what I did? You wouldn't believe this, but that's what I did. I swear to God and all the saints my mother believes in - I laughed.

I laughed, but it wasn't my voice. It was someone else's vocal

chords moving. Definitely it wasn't me. Why would I be laughing? It wasn't anything funny. It wasn't funny at all.

"You're pitiful," she blurted out, and ran away.

Time passed - between that moment, that day, and the day
she actually gave me back the ring - but I don't remember much
of it, because to tell you the truth, I was busy doing some first-
class drinking.

My mother came downstairs to talk to me one evening, when
all this was going on - I have an apartment in the basement of
her house. "What are you drinking?" she said. I knew she was trying to find a start, a way to begin.

"Martini," I said.

"Funny. That's what people used to drink years ago."

I didn't bother explaining to her that there had been a resur-
gence of the fancy gin and vermouth cocktail among people my
age. I didn't feel much like talking.

"No olive... I suppose fellows don't bother being fancy. I used
to like it with the olive. It wasn't a martini without it. Anyway,
you're a mess," she said.

Go tell her that... go tell it to Susan. This conversation was
with myself - my mother had nothing to do with it.

Hey. That sounds like a song. Go tell it to Susan. Maybe I
should be writing songs instead of stories. "Go tell it to..."

"Go tell it to the mountain... that you're a fool. Anyway, stop
drinking," she said. "You're going to ruin your life."

My mother is a sweetheart. Even when her words are harsh,
you can see oodles of caring on her face. And never mind her eyes.

So I say: "Mom, smile."

She winces instead.

Poor woman, doesn't know what to do with me.

Neither do my friends. I refuse to go out anywhere with

them anymore. And the people I work with, down at the car dealership, are really worried about me. I haven't sold a car in weeks. I used to be top salesperson there.

Anyway, I've got to tell you this, it's really important. It makes you see what a jerk I am. One day, at work, I saw this girl walking across the car lot, moving between cars, coming toward me. She looked so much like Susan from far away...

When she got close, I was shaking so bad it took several tries to shove my hands into my pockets.

"What's the matter with you," the pretty stranger said.

"Matter? Ugh... don't know. Something the matter?"

"Well, obviously," she said. "It's not hard to see. Anyway, the other fellow sent me over to you. I'm looking for a second-hand car that's not too old. He said you would help me... that you're the expert in that area."

Joe. Good old Joe. He had passed up a sale for himself to get me a customer. Between car salesmen that's as rare as roses blooming in winter. Outside in the freezing cold that is – in January.

Talk about Roses. Now that's something she loved. Susan I mean. Once I bought her a dozen yellow roses. Just out of the blue. Like that. Because I wanted to. Because she was beautiful.

"What's this for?" she said, her voice full of girlish surprise. Too girlish. I know that now. A put on reaction.

And how foolish do you think I should feel now, knowing that the day I gave her the roses, Susan had already missed her period once. She had been trying to get pregnant with me for over a year, but it didn't happen. So we were giving it a rest for a while. To see if it would help. We planned to have a baby first, get a house next, and then get married. Some of our friends had done that. As my mother says, doing things all turned around.

Anyway, where do you think the beautiful girl who wanted

to buy a car was all this time? Yes, you guessed it. She was standing there in the wind and the snow... waiting for an idiot salesman like me to stop talking in his head.

But then she left. The girl-customer I mean. She just turned around, shrugged, and left. And I was all alone.

"Hey. Wait!" I heard myself shout.

But she kept on going. She waved, yes, she did that. But it's how she did it that's important. Without turning around, she put her hand in the air and waved. And she said, "See you," in that tone that tells you exactly what she means. Like, see you in ten years, buddy. If you're lucky.

And Joe, good kind-hearted Joe, fatherly Joe, with four kids to support, almost tore his heart out when he found out I'd let the customer get away.

"You what?" he said, almost fainting right there in his old parka. "You fuckin' let her walk away!"

I just hung my head and let old Joe yell at me. What could I do? What can one do in life. Sometimes it's like that. Just out of your grasp. And if you think words are hard to put down on paper, a story difficult to tell, try to harness life... try to steer it down a rosy path. Try to shape it into a form. It just goddamn goes all over the place... hurting you as it drags itself slowly on top of you, like a bulldozer.

The House My Father Built

Y ou were always there, as far back as I can recall. You were
a bent old man, and I was a quiet little girl. I learned to walk
with my hands behind my back, the way you did, trying to keep
yourself straight and from leaning forward too much. You were
my father's father... but I could never imagine you looking tall
and straight like him, and with a full head of hair. You couldn't
have been so gentle then, since you would have had too many
responsibilities, still raising your own children. You didn't like
going to bed early. Maybe because it was not easy for you to lie
down, with your back so stiff and curved. How could you rest?
So you stayed up almost every night, enraging your wife so that
she yelled at you the next morning... Mama and Papa were always tired from working in the fields, and they often fell asleep
early, and I would stay up with you until the embers died in the
fireplace... or in the summer, when the dew began to dampen
our shoulders. We didn't really talk much, just words here and
there. Nothing in particular that I can remember. Sometimes you
said the rabbits needed more grass... or that the cherries were al-

most ripe... and sometimes you remembered the flood... I wanted you to talk more about that, but you wouldn't. I wanted you to tell me everything about that terrible spring, so that I could close my eyes before going to sleep, and see the muddy waters smoothing out the valley. But you would only mention that the sheep had all drowned, and then you drifted on to something else, as though out of habit. Just once you said it was good to be living up on a hill... and I know now you felt safe up there, where my father had built the new house, away from the path of the rolling water. How could I have known back then that down in the valley, when you would have heard the roar behind you, it would have been too late, for someone as bent as you to run. The water would have caught up to you - lucky when it happened they had warned you in time... But there are no hills in the land I live now, Nonno... and the house my father built is far away... You said the sheep had all drowned, young and old... there are no silences between us, just spaces between words.

Nothing Changes

The tree is ancient and the old man sleeps under it. He mostly sleeps there in the afternoon, and sometimes even in the evening when the heat is unbearable. Morning naps are rare. But today he can feel things starting out different. His limbs are heavy, his heart weak; his mind hazy. He has to close his eyes.

Right away he dreams. His dreams are always subtle; terrain and landscapes of the two greener seasons, floating by... and the gentler people that populate his life. Sometimes the stable animals, too; the cows and the donkey, the sheep. He never dreams of his wife.

Though sometimes when he's coming out of his dreams, but still hanging in the lull of sleep, he can see her at the window, watching him. Then he purposely keeps his eyes closed for a while longer, hoping she will go back into the inner part of the house, for mostly seeing her there is not just a dream, but something like a sixth sense, pupils of the mind.

"Old man," he now suddenly hears her shout. "What are you doing? It's only ten o'clock, and you're sleeping already. Come and start the fire! I have to get the food to the people in the field - have you forgotten?"

Carrying a bundle of kindling in his arms, he tries to pull himself up the stairs to the second floor of the house, for the stables are down below. He doesn't feel the pain in his back, not the way one feels a fresh pain. How many years has it been part of him? How many years... and how much more can nature curve his body... and how well nature has taken care of not breaking him in two, but mould and mould him to its own desired shape and twisted ending...

"Beat the eggs," she says, furious with him. "Beat! I can't be late! Not on a day like today, when you don't need to rub a match to make a flame. The world will burn with a sun like this.

Besides, they're late cutting the wheat - they're trying to hurry to catch up."

He picks up a fork and sits down with the bowl on his lap, starts mixing the heavy yolks. He has no strength in his arms, but it's only an omelet she's making, not a cake. The eggs mostly need to be blended.

"Whip!" she says. "What are you afraid of?"

His hand slows down. "What day is it today?"

She doesn't answer for a long time. But after she has flipped the omelette onto a plate, she pauses for a moment to straighten herself and rest. "You will see," she says to him. "You will see."

He watches her as she puts things into the wicker container: tablecloth, forks, a dishcloth; all the food she has prepared for the customary midmorning breakfast. Her breathing is heavy. Although younger by seven years, she too is old. What would he do if she died? Somehow God better be kind and settle him into a grave first.

She refuses to take the donkey, but carries the basket on her head, the way she has done for years. Only now he worries about her tripping on a stone or getting her foot caught in a stray vine as she makes her way downhill along footpaths and furrows.

"What day is it?" he asks again as she puts the load on her head, and straightens herself for the journey.

"Count," she says. "For once, count..."

Even in anger, she keeps her balance.

A tear sits at the corner of his eye. He can feel it there, like a soft bead. If he'll leave it alone, it'll remain there... and then when he's not thinking about it, it'll spread and dissolve, barely moistening his thin, thin lashes.

The sun is already a fireball in the sky, and it's not even noon yet. When she reaches the wheat field, she's ready to collapse but is careful not to show it. Her daughter-in-law comes to meet her and takes the load from her head. She carries it under the tree, where the others are already sitting, waiting.

The tree is skimpy, but it's the only one there. A frail covering of shade is better than no shade at all. There's no source of water nearby, not a spring nor a river, where they can go and cool themselves. She has brought them a jug of water, but they'll need that to wash down the dust from their throats... and take some of their thirst away. Nobody asks what day it is. Not like that fool up at the house.

An automobile is heard coming along the valley road. All morning only a truck has passed by on its way to the next town. They all know it's too early... but eyes turn anyway. They all watch Letizia...

"The sickle," says Letizia's husband, suddenly jumping up. "It's dull. Christ, can't we have some sharp sickles for once?"

"Sit down and eat, Amedeo, before the food is gone," says the son. "I sharpened the sickles last night. I did them all. Nothing wrong with your sickle."

Letizia brings her hand to her temple, touches a strand of hair that has come out from underneath her kerchief. She doesn't tuck it back in, but twists and rolls it, winding it tight like a thread.

"I'll show you how to sharpen a sickle," says Amedeo, wiping sheets of sweat from his forehead. The anger on his neck is turning purple.

"I'll take the bloody thing to my house and show you. I'll show everyone!"

"Amedeo," warns the other man, a neighbour. "Where are you going? Nothing changes. Too sharp a blade is no good. Think of fingers missing from your hands... blood that doesn't need to be shed... "

But Amedeo can't be stopped. He's already hurrying across the field, the sickle like a wild banner in his hand.

"Let him go," says the son. "Let him go. We've done all we can. Maybe it's better this way."

Letizia gets up from the ground. She takes her kerchief off her head, wipes her neck with it, the perspiration down in her breasts.

She will not speak. She never does.

"He'll come back," says the daughter-in-law. "Amedeo will come back."

"Yes," says the other woman, the neighbour's wife. "He'll cool off from the cool water in the house."

"Yes, you will see," says the daughter-in-law.

Letizia lifts her head and slowly starts walking along the edge of the field. Her head is bare now and her hair is slowly spreading across her shoulders. She ties her kerchief around her waist... and swings her long, flared skirt back and forth, brushing it past her legs. The last they see is the way she kicks her shoes off, and throws them in the ditch.

The neighbour's wife looks around at all the others. "Did you see that? Did you see the way she was acting... and she was singing... did you hear how she was singing..."

"Shut up," says the daughter-in-law. "It's time we minded our own business. "Maybe she's doing it for all of us. Maybe she's doing it for Amedeo, too. After all, how can a sharecropper's wife turn down a landlord?"

"A kick in the balls," says the neighbour's wife, but her words are barely a whisper - she's not convinced.

"Talk... talk. We're all good for talk. But do you remember what happened in the other town... when five families were taken away from the land? They had to go back south to the mountains and scrape a living from the rocks. This is good land... and the houses are like mansions, compared to what we used to have. We could all be replaced with the snap of a finger."

The two men are very silent. They have dark clouds in their eyes; it's hard to read their minds.

The old lady gathers the forks, folds the tablecloth. "I'll take Letizia's place in the fields. This work has to be done."

"You'll do no such thing," snaps the son. "And don't argue. That's all we need on a day like today, to have to pick you up from the ground... and who do you think is going to run to get the doctor, with the world burning up..."

"Yes, do as you're told," says the daughter-in-law. "Letizia will be back tomorrow... Amedeo, too."

At home the old lady tries to sleep, but her eyes just won't close. She can't even rest on a chair; she can't sit still. She feels the pumping of her own heart...

Going to the window, she opens the shutters. Slowly begins to undo her bun, loosening the long thin strands of gray hair. She picks up the honey-coloured comb from the window sill, and holds it in her hand... watches the old man sleeping under the big tree. She wonders what it would be like to put her hand on his forehead, to touch him once more before one of them is going to die...

The old man is dreaming. He's dreaming a river shaped like a sickle. A small river, where thatched, sun-burned grass is cooling into the water, along the edges. But is it a dream, for he knows he's not quite asleep yet...? It's really more like an image, a flicker of familiar landscape and terrain... and an old woman at the window, getting ready to call his name...

A Garden of Soft Colours

S arnia. I am not fond of travelling anymore. It's not that I am scared of flying or anything like that, but I am getting old and I like being in my own house. I am happy watching the TV shows that I like, and at night I rejoice lying in my own bed. It's summer and I can putter in my garden, growing tomatoes, beans, and cucumbers, and looking after my flowers around the house. But my husband says that we should go over one more time. He doesn't insist, but still he keeps mentioning it every day.

"Orlando," I say to him. "Why do you want us to go back there again? Your family is all gone, and my sister is dead, too. There's her children and her grandchildren, but that's not the same."

He doesn't answer, but I can tell he's not done with it. He'll come back to it some other time; for now he's just letting it rest. So the next morning when he brings it up again, I am not at all surprised. He says he's not talking about going to Italy, but to France.

"You still have your brother there. He's still alive," he says. "You should go and see him. You shouldn't just forget like that."

Airport in Toronto. Orlando thinks I never loved my brother

Salvatore. But that's not true. Well, maybe it is true, but somehow it's not right. He shouldn't say that. I did care for him as much as I could, after all he was eighteen when I was born. And isn't caring a form of love, too? But I know what Orlando means. He means I wasn't close to him the way I was to the other four brothers. The one in California, and the one in Vancouver, who both died in the last three years; and the other two, who died young, during the last war - one buried in some town we don't even know in Greece, the other in Italy in the place where we were born.

On the plane to France. I guess I loved my sister the most. Maybe because she was a girl and we could do things together when we were young. We were only two years apart and that made us almost like twins. She was not as strong as I was and I always helped her finish the chores that my father assigned to her. We all had to work very hard to keep our small farm productive. We were never really short of food, but whatever my mother put on the table was always gone in two minutes. Five healthy young men; they would eat everything so fast. "Leave some food for your little sister," my mother would cry. "She has to grow, too!" But usually by the time my mother said that, it was too late. The bowls were already empty.

Still on the plane. They phoned in the middle of the night. Five years ago. Her son spoke; he was all broken up. He said to me, "Oh Zia Giulia... I have really bad news. We lost my mother - she is gone." Poor Gina, she was in the hospital recovering from an operation, a major operation, but not anything unusual. She was going to be all right. But then a blood clot. Thrombosis. "Just like that," her son said. I went back to bed and stared at the dark ceiling. Orlando was asleep. He never wakes up when the phone rings at night. He takes the sleeping pills the doctor prescribed for him. So I didn't tell anyone about my sister until morning. What was the use of waking anyone up? We all must die. No use making too much fuss. But people can't believe I am like that. Often I have to explain to friends that when you've been through a war, when you have seen so much pain, so much suffering, it isn't easy to cry anymore. The tears just don't come. That's the way it is. But I used to save food for her, so I know what she meant to me. I would hide it before the boys would eat it all. A rabbit leg, a piece of sausage, a chunk of corn bread, and when there was baking, a cookie or a piece of cake. "You're still giving me things," she said the last time I went to Italy to see her. It was the day I was going back to Canada, and I was leaving her all the dresses I had brought with me, for her to keep. The wash and wear ones she liked so much. "You still think about me," she said. "You still never forget me."

Paris. His daughter has come to get us. There was room in the car but he didn't come. We didn't expect him to, he's eighty-six. Maybe he won't even recognize us. The last time he wrote, about two years ago, he said he was starting to forget things. His handwriting was still perfect. Still, he said his memory was not the same anymore. I can't believe how he always wrote such beautiful letters. I don't know where he learned to write like that. The handwriting almost like professional calligraphy. Like the rest of us, he only went to school for two years. What can you learn in two years? We weren't allowed to stay in school longer than that, because we had to stay home and work the land. It was the land that gave us food… but of course it didn't give us money. Oh, maybe a bit here and there, when we took from our mouths so we could go and sell at the market. A few dozen eggs, some beans, the odd chicken, some milk from our two cows. But not enough. Never enough. That's why we all left. That's why we all went to other countries. Emigrated. To have more than just food. To give our children more than two years of schooling. Left our parents, our place of birth.

Gina was the only one who stayed back there. Of course, nobody encouraged her to leave. We all felt she wasn't as strong as the rest of us. Not strong enough to go and live outside her own country. We were afraid she couldn't take the hardships everyone encountered at the beginning, the first few years. And really, she was happy enough staying there, for every year or every second year one of us would go back to visit her. We always made sure of that. We didn't want her to be sad. We wanted to see her happy - we didn't want her to feel left behind.

Villejuif. We are sitting in the garden, Salvatore and me. A little wooden bench he had made a long time ago, for his wife to sit on and crochet under the shade. Now his wife doesn't crochet anymore. Her eyes aren't what they used to be anymore. So she stays in the house all day, never wanting to go outside... but he still likes to come to the garden. He's a short little man, but his back is still straight, his shoulders square. He's not bent at all like most old people. He carries a cane all the time, but I am not sure why - his eyes are all right. In fact, he doesn't even need to wear glasses. But maybe he's afraid of losing his balance. I don't blame him. I know I am always afraid of falling, of breaking a hip, so easily done at our age. So there we are, Salvatore and me... not looking at each other. We're both staring ahead... but with the corner of my eye I can see his eyebrows. Two salt and pepper peaks. I think of the mountains enclosing the valley where we were born... We sit silent for a long time. Then finally he speaks. He says: "I thought we said good-bye the last time you came..." I am not sure if he's annoyed with me or just trying to be witty. He has always been a little different than the rest of us. Even when he was young, you never knew if he was being serious or not. We used to always get so angry with him. But now at my age anger is a forgotten passion. I don't even get angry with Orlando anymore. I have no problem letting things ride.

Time is too precious to be wasted on anger. So I laugh, instead. I laugh, gently, and tell him it wasn't my idea to come. "Blame Orlando," I tell him. "Orlando wanted to come, so that he could see the Eiffel Tower one more time."

A restaurant in Villejuif. There's eight of us at the table. Salvatore and his wife; Orlando and me; and there's Salvatore's daughter and her husband and their two children. We're all holding menus in front of us. Busy reading, deciding what to order. But strange, when I look up, I see my brother looking at me, and there are tears running down his cheeks. His daughter notices, and I can see she doesn't know why he's crying. I don't either, but I would like to think it's because he'll never see me again. Because this is truly the last time we will be together. But I am not sure. Most likely that's not the reason. Maybe it doesn't even have anything to do with being sad. Maybe it has to do with the lapses of memory he mentioned in his last letter. Who knows. Maybe he's just crying because it's his birthday.

In the Garden the next day. "I was the oldest of the boys and you the older of the girls. And here we are both still alive," he says. I wish I could touch his hand or something. But we can't do a thing like that. With the other brothers it was so easy, but not with Salvatore. "Why did you stop writing," I ask him. "It had nothing to do with your mind - I know. You're not anywhere near being senile." He shrugs... and there's a bit of devilry in his eyes. "I guess I wanted it to end when I could still explain it to you. I didn't want it to happen and not know that it had happened."

I laugh. "Oh, Salvatore... you think of these things too much. You will probably walk to your grave with still the stride of a young man." He laughs, too. "Well, I walked all the way from our village to Paris. That was a good stretch of road, Giulia. A real long stretch of road." I shake my head. I had forgotten that. He had left

131

home with a knapsack on his back and two extra pair of shoes hanging from a string around his neck. There was no money for the train and he was too proud to borrow from anyone. It took him four months to get there.

The last day before going back. It's hard to believe Salvatore has gone down so much in a week. The doctor said he caught some kind of bug, and at his age it's not easy to shake it. He's usually very meticulous about his appearance, but this morning the side part of his hair is not straight, and the peaks of his eyebrows have not been smoothed in place. And he seems to need the cane. Holding it in front of him, he relies on it for strength, even though he's sitting down. "Are you happy?" he says, hiding his resentfulness. "This is what you always wanted, isn't it? To see me weak like this..." Strangely, I am not surprised he has said that. Maybe I expected it all along. And now it has come out at last... I cross my arms and don't say anything for a long time, but I know that sooner or later I'll have to answer him. And in time I do. Sighing, I say, "You have never been able to forgive me, have you...?" He rests both hands on his cane. "Why should I forgive you... you have done nothing." I stand up and walk around smelling the roses for a while - his garden is full of roses. He had always loved roses. After he went away from Italy, my mother used to say, "Who will look after my roses now that Salvatore is gone?"

Still in the garden. I guess we're ready to talk at last. We just have to, we can't die and take this thing to the grave with us. This bitterness. Like poison from a snake bite, it has to be drawn out. "You were the oldest," I say. "And you knew your responsibilities... you didn't leave home and get married until we were all grown up. You stayed to help the parents. You were always so strong... you always did what needed to be done. And you cared for Gina, I know you cared for her a lot. But me... since the day the neighbour's son blew himself up with that hand grenade, things changed. Didn't they, Salvatore?" He doesn't answer. But slowly, very slowly, he stands up. He paces around for quite a while. "You see all my roses," he says at last, extending his hand toward them. "Every colour but red. Red is not an easy colour, Giulia... Yes, I was strong and tried to take care of everybody. And I was the one who was expected to pick him up... but I couldn't. I just couldn't. But you did, you put him back together the best you could for his parents. You did it, Giulia. You did it."

I close my eyes tight. I don't want to remember, and I force it all back, way back, where I hope it'll never try to come out again. I know I couldn't handle remembering things like that anymore. I used to, for many years it was all so alive in my mind. But now my heart is frail and I know what it can take and what it can't. So I make myself stare at the roses. White and yellow ones. Soft colours... a garden of soft colours. But then my eyes get blurry and I can't see anymore. I am crying, I must be. My eyes are wet and I have nothing to dry myself with. But after a while, Salvatore touches my arm and hands me his handkerchief. Confused, I don't know what to do, what to say.

I should say thank you, but I can't. But some words do come out after a long time. "We all loved Gina, didn't we, Salvatore?" I say. He nods and looks away. "Yes, it was easy to love Gina... she was not as strong as the rest of us." And to my surprise, he slowly hangs his cane on the branch of a pear tree for a minute, to test his balance. There's a sad look on his face, but at the same time, he seems like he's going to be all right.

On the plane back to Canada. Orlando holds my hand for a minute. He says something has happened to me. He's not used to seeing me so quiet. He wants to know what I am thinking. So I tell him about Salvatore. "He has promised to come and visit us in

Canada," I tell him. Orlando can't believe it. "Do you think he really will?" he says. "Besides, do you think he can make the trip?" I think about it for a minute, and I know it doesn't really matter if he really comes or not. It's his saying it that counts. "Oh, he might," I say, smiling. "He might come." Orlando settles back in his seat. "Good. Finally the man knows whose turn it is." I look at my husband and realize that all these years he's probably been angry with Salvatore for not having ever come to Canada to visit me. So I know the time has come for me to tell Orlando the truth... to explain to him the way things really were between Salvatore and me. But not now, he has just closed his eyes to rest, and I won't bother him. Later, I mustn't forget. Orlando has always been a good man.

Home. I am in my back yard and I am singing softly. It is almost the beginning of winter and I am cleaning out the vegetable garden. Orlando and I didn't eat even half of the vegetables I grew. So much abundance in this country... so much gone to waste. I usually freeze the beans, but this year I couldn't. They got too hard while we were away. But that's all right. I don't mind. I am glad Orlando talked me into going to France. I did tell him finally, a few days ago, that the whole thing wasn't all Salvatore's fault. In fact, maybe it wasn't his fault at all. "I was the one who was bitter," I said to Orlando. I guess I just couldn't forgive him for being weak - for not being able to stand blood. For *making me be the one who had to do it.* And Salvatore knew. That's why he never came to Canada to see me. He kept in touch with letters, but he never once came to my house. How could he, when my door was not really truly open for him? He *knew* how I felt deep down; he knew how I felt about him all along. He told me all these things before we left France. Yes, we talked... at last we talked. He said we all make our choices in life... and sometimes those choices are not easy to live with. He said I always wanted to be strong. I wanted to be stronger than the boys. And I guess, in a way, I turned out to be the strongest of all in our family. But I paid my price. Orlando could tell you. Orlando knows the nightmares I used to have when I was younger. But thank God, the years make everything easier. Somehow, the years lay a cushion on everything... that's truly a blessing.

Ant Hills

I was in a book store looking at an archaeology book when a male voice at my side said, "You sure are a reader of heavy stuff."

Expecting it to be an old friend whose voice I didn't recognize, I turned, ready to greet him pleasantly.

"Hi," he grinned, ignoring the surprised look on my face. I had never seen the guy before.

Confused, I closed the book in my hand, closing the page upon the picture of a skeleton from another civilization. "I was trying to find a book for a friend - a gift," I said, lying.

What reason I had to want to cover up my interest in the life and cultures of ancient peoples I don't know, but I should have ignored him and walked away. I was not in the habit of letting strangers come on to me like that.

I placed the book back onto the shelf and moved further along the aisle. He followed me, keeping a polite distance.

"I bet you're really the one who seeks details in ancient bones - not your friend," he laughed.

Since he was a stranger, I should have been thinking he was

bold and arrogant, but he wasn't like that at all. He just had this blunt and different way with words, but his eyes were gentle.

"How do you know?" I asked.

He stepped back and surveyed me carefully. "Uh, let me see. I would say it's the way you have your hair… pulled so tight to the back of your head."

"Maybe I am a ballerina," I said.

"Naw," he pondered. "You're not fluid enough to spin on your toes."

"Thanks."

"There you go… letting your feelings get hurt."

Sighing, I turned and looked right at him. "What do you want? Why did you follow me?"

"I didn't," he said softly.

I hadn't expected our eyes to meet like that. He was the one to look away first. "We came in the door at the same time," he said, leafing through a magazine on the shelf. "I thought it was some kind of *sign*."

I glanced toward the front of the store. There was no door - the whole store opened up onto the mall's corridor. "Thirty feet wide - sure. A sign of what, may I ask?"

"There!" he beamed. "You should smile like that all the time. A bit on the shy side, but perfect."

I had not smiled at all.

He was tall and slim of muscle. His kinky red hair softened by streaks of gray. He looked about my age, forty.

"You didn't answer my question - the *sign*?"

"Promise not to laugh."

"All right. Tell me."

"A sign that we share the same secret passion for ice cream."

I tried not to laugh.

"I knew I was right," he exclaimed. "I knew it!"

"Do you ever give up?" I said, moving on.

I am a fast walker, but he managed to catch up to me a few stores away. "Eh, wait! Give me a chance... allow me to introduce myself. I am Tony - "

"I am Marguerite - and I am married."

"I know," he said, looking at my hand. "But I am harmless."

• • •

The lady at the ice cream store was really friendly. She was amused at our bantering and smiled at us. She tried to fill our order, but when she couldn't get it right, she shook her head, giving up. "Listen, you two happy souls," she laughed. "I just can't get three scoops to stay on these cones. How about two and some?"

Tony said, "Just great - thanks for trying." He insisted on paying her for three scoops anyways.

My husband and I often walk by ice cream places. We always look, but neither one of us ever suggests stopping.

We were near the exit of the mall, and we went out to the parking lot. It was a hot day, and the ice cream kept melting fast. Tony had no problem, but I ran out of Kleenexes, trying to catch the drips from the cone.

"Weren't you ever a kid?" he teased, seeing how slow I was at licking. He handed me his handkerchief.

I had been a kid all right, only no one had ever bought me treats. I had been raised by a mean stepfather and a mother who drank herself to death. But I wasn't going to tell Tony all that. I just shrugged.

Our cars were parked close by, and we tried to stretch the distance by walking slowly, stopping completely at times.

"Listen Marguerite," he said. "What are we going to do about us? I know it was crazy, the way I came up to you. I don't usually go around doing this sort of thing. But something made me do it today, as soon as I saw you. It was instant, something pulling me. But it's really your move now... you're the one who's tied down."

On the cement in front of us, an ant, in her hurry to get away, zigzagged wildly, before disappearing into the grass at the edge of the parking lot.

Two nights ago my husband squirted drops of poison all around our yard. Before leaving the house this morning, I looked. The ant hills were deserted.

"The earth is so dry," I murmured.

"And cracked. Some rain would do it good... with lots of thunder."

I folded his handkerchief neatly into a square. I gave it back to him, saying "Thanks."

He wrapped the handkerchief around his index finger. The finger looked bandaged. It made me laugh.

"I cheered you up," he said. "I made those old bones shake away from your mind... doesn't that count for anything?"

I nodded, unable to speak. I desperately wanted him to hold me in his arms - I could tell he'd be gentle and caring. But he didn't make any move at all, not even to touch my hand. Maybe he knew what was best in the long run.

"Well," he said, and shrugged. Then he added, "Well *what?*"

I remained silent for a minute. Then, taking a deep breath, I said, "How about me going to the left and you to the right?"

"Right," he smiled.

"Right," I tried to smile back.

"No, it's left for you... but you're catching on fast."

We both laughed a little too loud.

Then he did it beautifully. He pivoted around and headed the other direction, his arm waving behind him.

I started waving back, but immediately realized how futile it was, for he was looking straight ahead.

In the wake of my abandoned gesture, my hand fell... and slowly began searching my face. I could feel the bones firmly curving beneath my cheek. I traced the frame of my jaw... then, slowly into the cushion of my chin.

When faced with painful moments, I always felt the need to ponder the existence of lasting things, hoping to discover some suggestion of survival.

Another Time, Another Day

Anna rises slowly from the bed and goes to the window to look outside. As the years have gone by, this seems to have become a morning ritual for her, just after getting up. Their bedroom is on the second floor of the house and from there she has a perfect view. A view that is beautiful every season. It's something she can count on day in and day out. Something simple, slightly magic at times… a bit lonely and desolate other times, but nevertheless dependable.

"Did it snow?" Giuseppe asks from beneath the blankets. She didn't know he had been awake and she envies how he can lie there, eyes closed, just enjoying the warmth of the bed. She herself is always restless in bed.

Anna nods. "It snowed all right. It must have come down all night."

They are late risers and the sun is already high in the sky. The hills gleam as though sprinkled with a thousand chips of diamonds. And the tall evergreens in the bush to the east of the house send back a blue transparency toward the sky. It's going to be a beautiful day, she thinks.

Then just like that, not knowing exactly what has moved her to it, she turns to her husband and says, "Giuseppe, I don't want to leave this place…"

First he laughs at her earnestness, her seriousness. Then after a while, when she has almost given up expecting a response of any sort, he says, "I didn't know we were going anywhere."

She looks at him and shakes her head. Most of her married life, and there has been a lot of it, she has cringed at her husband's helpless attempts at humour. But on a bad day she would not put his answers in the category of humour at all. On a bad day, she always feels he is simply being sarcastic. But what is the use of despairing over it - the man will never change. He just has no grace with words.

And that certain *reaching* has never been there either. Or, perhaps, had she missed it? Or had she expected too much, she wondered, recalling what a friend had told her once. She had said, "You know, Anna, men have their own way of seeing things, which has nothing to do with women or how women feel."

So Anna cannot, and will not dispose of what has been there. Of what has been good. Of her good fortune that many people would envy. Of the stability… faithfulness and accountability. All those good, solid things, for after all so much has been satisfactory in their marriage.

But all this reasoning, this acceptance, doesn't necessarily stop her from going back into the past, into each day, each month, each year… into each moment wrapped up into sequences of memories. It doesn't stop her from searching, from defining, from trying to awaken something that through some excusable fault of her own she has missed. Some ultimate beauty. A revelation maybe.

"Giuseppe," she says, looking right at him. She wants to explain herself in a way that he might finally, at last, in his years of aging, be trapped into listening, into hearing what she really has to say. "You know, that's not *really* what I meant."

"What did you mean then?"

"I meant... I meant I don't want to die."

"Well, we all have to go. Don't you think that's the way it is?"

Angry, more angry than perhaps she's ever been in her whole life, because now there's the added hopelessness of knowing he'll never ever change, something she's really known all along but has stubbornly refused to accept. And then the actual threat of one's extinction coming nearer and nearer as the years she may have left, if it is to be years, are like a distance that can be easily measured. Just a little stretch of road left in the journey.

"And what can I say to that?" she murmurs, taking a deep breath before sitting down on the edge of the bed to get dressed. "So you have discovered America, Giuseppe. Now that is something."

Couldn't he have just said something like "Are you okay, Anna? What's the matter, dear?" And hearing those tender words of concern, she may even have eased her body, full of arthritis as it was, back into bed, just to stay at his side for a few more minutes. They could have held each other for a moment... not for too long, because being squeezed was painful for her now. Still, she could have told him when to stop... and then another time, another day they could have tried again.

"I know I didn't discover America... but you come out with some things that I don't know what to tell you."

As if there was to be *telling*, she thinks, pushing her slippers with her cane to bring them closer to her feet, where she can just slip into them. *Oh thanks be to God for a good strong cane. It serves many purposes. These days one sure needs all the help one can get.*

But on a day like today, her heart is feeling particularly soft over things she cannot quite put her finger on... perhaps things of loss over the years, missed opportunities that might not actually ever have been there anyway... tender moments so sweet that deep down she can actually, sensibly, put aside as day dreams. Yes, on a day like today, all of these things gathered into a sensation of tender pain, and that's when she *knew* she had wanted more. Not anything different, but just a little more. Like someone coming toward you just to touch your hurt, your tender spots, so that you may touch back and say, "Yes, I feel. I too feel... I feel your pain, and together we'll rise above it."

The Last Time

It was the first day I was completely on my own as the new owner of the Corner Variety. The store was to be my livelihood from now on and I was pleasant to everyone, smiling a lot. But from the moment I saw her, I knew she wasn't the smiling type, though it seemed to please her that I was cheerful.

"You bought this store?" she asked right off.

"Yes," I said, handing her the change for a litre of milk. "That I did."

"You think you'll make money?"

I chuckled. "Oh, I don't know. I hope to make a living at it. I had to do something. I am a carpenter - still a few years before I can draw a pension. Not much work in construction these days."

She nodded, agreeing. "Yeah, nobody's building anything here anymore."

She wasn't in a hurry to leave. I wanted to say something else to her, but I couldn't. I could go only so far with small talk, and then I hoped the customer would leave.

I wasn't hoping that with her, though. It was the opposite. Still, I was tongue-tied.

"I'd better go," she sighed. "I was working all day - ten hours. I am a cook. Some days I get pretty tired."

"Nasty out there tonight," I managed to call out, as she went out the door.

The front of the store was one big glass panel, and I was able to watch her walk across the road. A strong north wind was blowing, but it didn't seem to bother her at all. She seemed made to walk in the wind. She was small and compact. Made of iron, so to speak. She had nothing on her head, except a headband to keep her steel-gray hair back. She was wearing tight stretch pants and her boots came up to her knees. Her black leather jacket was quite short. I thought about her small behind freezing in that bitter cold... but really, I knew she was all right.

Later, I wondered about her age. She could have been anywhere from fifty to seventy. It was hard to tell. Her face had no wrinkles, but her skin was a hard brown.

Each day I looked for her to come back. Some nights I even looked out my bedroom window, in the apartment above the store, hoping to see her walking by. She was the kind of woman most men would never look at a second time... but for some strange reason she excited me a lot.

When she came back, several weeks later, at first I didn't even know she was in the store. Suddenly she was there, next in line, handing me a five dollar bill for a loaf of bread. I laughed like a nervous boy, and I felt a flush on my face. I was glad I had a long beard to hide it.

"And how are you tonight?" I asked, trying to sound natural.

"Not bad. Fine."

She had a peculiar way of looking in a vague direction while speaking, and then right into your face in time to catch your response.

"How is work?"

"Busy. Too much. And on my day off, I don't even have ten minutes to rest. So much to do at home."

"It's a tough world, isn't it?"

She stood aside to let a young man pay for his cigarettes, then she came back in front of the counter to talk. "This world is nothing but trouble. Trouble from when you're born till you die."

She sounded so unhappy. Her eyes were a nice brown, but her pupils were so small...

How I longed to touch and caress her hard brown skin... her softness was all inside. I leaned over the counter.

She drew back. The phone rang, and a number of customers came in all at once. In the midst of the commotion, I didn't see her leave.

At night I couldn't sleep anymore. I tossed and turned until it was almost time to get up.

There were a lot of Italian people in the neighbourhood who came in regularly, and often I was tempted to ask them if they knew her. But I never did. She could be somebody's sister or mother... somebody's wife. I didn't want to bring her any trouble.

As for me, I had been separated for over thirty years. I was free.

Weeks went by and no sign of her. I bought myself a bottle of brandy and kept it by the bed. I needed to get my rest and be able to work the long hours - I couldn't afford to hire help.

When I finally saw her again, several months had gone by, and I had been drinking more than eating.

"You don't look good. What's wrong? You sick?" I was accustomed to her bluntness.

"Oh no," I stammered. "I'm fine. Actually, I feel great - I just wanted to lose some weight." I put my hands behind my back so she wouldn't see them shaking.

"Why you want to lose weight? You're crazy!"

Laughing softly, I leaned over the counter. "I haven't seen you for a long time," I said, looking at her.

"I was busy. We had to fix the house... to sell it. We moved to an apartment. My husband, he decided. Nothing changed his mind."

"That's too bad," I said, with feeling.

She was hanging on to the strap of her shoulder purse with both hands. "Someday I'll jump from the balcony."

In her strange, controlled desperation, she excited me even more. I knew what it would be like making love to her. I wouldn't be surprised if the sheets would be stained with blood when it was over. She would be like a young girl the first time... I leaned as close to her as I could, with the counter between us.

"Apartments can be very lonely places."

I hadn't expected her lips to tremble like that, and I became giddy, intoxicated. My laughter was like dry sobs. I knew about the tears in my eyes only when I felt their wetness slide down my cheeks.

I was reaching out to touch her face when suddenly our privacy was shattered by a delivery man coming in.

I was so upset by the intrusion that for a minute everything in front of me went black. I closed my eyes to get a grip on myself. But by the time I was able to see again, she was already going out the door.

That was the last time I saw her.

I am on pension now, and I could sell the store and retire, but I won't. I'll be here behind this counter for as long as my health holds. I am still hoping she'll stop by again someday... when she needs a loaf of bread or something.

ACKNOWLEDGEMENTS

"Cinzia" appeared in *Sweet Lemons: Writings with a Sicilian Accent*, Legas, 2004; in *Beneath the Surface*, McMaster University Society of English, 2000; and in *Bibliosofia, Letteratura Canadese e altre culture*, 2006.

"The Blue House" appeared in *Strange Peregrinations: Italian Canadian Literary Landscapes*, The Frank Iacobucci Centre For Italian Canadian Studies, University of Toronto, 2007; in *Accenti Magazine*, Issue 11, July 2007; and in *Nutshell Quarterly*, 1990.

"Abandoned Wedding Ring" appeared in *The Lakeshore Advance*, Volume 18, No. 8, 2001; and in *The Many Faces of Woman*, River City Press, 2002.

"A Little Visiting" appeared *Sands of Huron*, River City Press, 1990; and under the title "Filippo Antico" in *Solstice: The Truth and Fictions of Ageing*, A Special Issue of the *Prairie Journal of Canadian Literature*, edited by A. Burke.

"Blueberry Muffins" appeared in *The Ecphorizer*, 1987; and as a revised version in *The First Person*, 1990; and in *Voices of the Rapids*, River City Press, 1993.

"Before You Leave" appeared in *The White Crow*, 1997.

"Call Display" appeared in *Accenti Magazine*, March 2003.

"Don't Forget Tomorrow" appeared in *Pleiades*, 1998.

"Faces in the Window" appeared in *Mind in Motion*, 1985; and in *Flare Up*, River City Press, 1983.

"No Man of Music" appeared in *Timber Creek Review*, 1999.

"Nothing Changes" appeared in *In all Directions*, Fitzhenry & Whiteside, 2000; in *The Dynamics of Cultural Exchange*, Cusmano, 2002.

"Talk About Roses" appeared in the *White Crow*, Issue 2, Vol. 4, 1999.

"The Last Frozen Dinner" appeared in the anthology *The Many Faces of Woman*, edited by Marisa De Franceschi, River City Press, 2001.

"Snow on the Roofs" in *The Exphorizer*, Number 62, 1987; in the *Paper Bag* and in the *AICW Newsletter*, 1999; in *Bluewater Tidings*, CAA Sarnia Branch Newsletter, Sept 1997.

"Fast Forward" appeared in *Accenti Magazine*, Winter 2006; and in *Writing Beyond History*, 2006; in *Bibliosofia, Letteratura Canadese e altre culture*, 2007.

"A Garden of Soft Colours" appeared in *Zymergy Literary Review*, Vol. V, Autumn 1991.

"The Last Time" appeared in *Bibliosofia, Letteratura Canadese e altre culture*, Aug. 2006.

"A Place I Once Knew" appeared in *Bibliosofia, Letteratura Canadese e altre culture*, 2006.

"Before the Roses Fade" appeared in *Bibliosofia, Letteratura Canadese e altre culture*, 2006.